Survivors

By Zion Ben Jonah

www.jesuschristians.com

Box A678
Sydney South 1235
Australia

Printed by Printshop
Chennai, South India

From Zion Ben-Jonah

My real name is not Zion Ben-Jonah, and the characters in this book are not real people. In fact, the whole story is fiction. Much of what it conveys is total conjecture.

Zion Ben-Jonah is inspired by a character in a series of books by Tim LaHaye and Jerry Jenkins. In that series, a character named Tsion Ben-Judah sets the world straight at a time when the mass media is monopolised by materialistic forces that seek to distort the truth.

We believe that this is already the situation in the world of religious entertainment. In order for a book to sell in a really big way, certain important truths (truths which are uncomfortable, and hard for the masses to accept) must be left out.

In the tradition of LaHaye's Tsion Ben-Judah, we will include those truths in this account of what we believe is coming to pass shortly, in America and elsewhere around the world.

Almost certainly some of what it predicts will *not* happen exactly as it is described in this book. This book is not meant to be taken as a prophecy in itself. But it *is* an attempt to *apply* the prophecies of the Bible to modern day events. A discerning reader will need to determine what is factual and what is not, as the actual events unfold in the years ahead.

Discovering the whole truth often involves knowing and admitting the limits of our understanding. We are each trapped within the boundaries of our own experience and imagination. No one has total knowledge of all truth except God himself. There will, I believe, be truth in this book which you have never read elsewhere. It is my firm conviction that I have been inspired by God as I have written it. But I (or anyone else) can be *inspired* in what I (or they) say, without being *infallible*. If you keep that in mind, you will be able to maintain better perspective as you read through what I have written.

On the other hand, I have a responsibility (as does every other Christian) not to deliberately distort truth for selfish motives. I could (as others have done) make millions of dollars by altering the facts in order to give the public what they want to hear. This book will not do that.

Instead, it will try to tell you what you *need* to know in order to be prepared for what is almost certainly going to happen on earth in the next few years, whether what it says sells or not. I have done it in story form, but I have also tried to be true to what the Bible actually says about the future, whether it conforms with popular opinion or not. These issues are too serious for anyone to take a chance on leading people astray just to make a few more dollars.

Notes appear at the end of each chapter to help you understand points made in that chapter. Those notes are my comments on the biblical implications of that part of the story.

4   TABLE OF CONTENTS

BOOK ONE

BOOK TWO

BOOK THREE

BOOK ONE
1. Left Behind

Everyone was caught off guard when the trouble began. But no one was more unprepared than those who supposedly knew ahead of time what was to happen.

Rayford Strait was not a believer, so he never expected any of this -- not in his lifetime, nor in anyone else's lifetime. But he was a realist. If circumstances changed (as they had as a result of the attack), then he would simply make the necessary adjustments and set about doing what needed to be done. Which is more or less what he did.

His wife and son, on the other hand, were believers. Irene Strait attended church faithfully, not far from where they lived, in Prospect Heights, Illinois. Vernon Billings, Irene's pastor at New Hope Chapel, often taught about the troubles that were going to come on the earth. He had a shelf full of books and even video tapes detailing what to expect. The topic had become something of an obsession with him.

Irene knew from what she had heard at New Hope Chapel, that a popular world leader was going to arise who would gain control over the entire planet. She had heard that he would persecute believers on a scale never before known. She knew that there would be death and destruction everywhere, and that her own country would not be spared.

Irene had shared much of this with her 13 year old son, Raymie. She tried to share it with her 19-year-old daughter, Chloe, too, but Chloe was -- like her father -- a cynic. She had little interest in anything she could not see and touch.

Raymie found the books, the lectures, and especially the videos exciting. They were scary at times, but he took comfort in the fact that he would never have to go through what they were describing, because he would be whisked up to heaven before it all started... instantly and painlessly... and all because he had said a little prayer asking Jesus into his heart. Raymie faithfully prayed for his father and his sister, that they too would say the prayer before it was too late. If only they would, then they could all go to heaven together.

Irene prayed the same prayer that Raymie prayed, and she prayed it even more faithfully and more fervently than Raymie did. She did not want any member of her family to be left behind. But she never for a moment thought that she or Raymie would be among those who would be left. She had books and tapes and videos and a long list of religious experts to back her up in her belief that she and others like her would be spared.

All of the suffering, she had been told, was reserved for someone else, for someone more appropriately suited to suffering... like the Jews. After all, they have had more *practice* than the rest of us when it comes to suffering!

Rayford Strait was piloting an early morning flight from London to Chicago on a Tuesday in May when the invasion began. He had left London at 5am and was about halfway to Chicago when he received word from Civil Aviation authorities in Chicago that unauthorised traffic had been picked up on radar in Canada, and it was crossing his proposed flight path. (It was about 3:30am in Chicago by that time.)

At first Rayford had been asked to divert to another corridor, but while they were still communicating the details, another message came through as an all frequencies broadcast. A distraught flight controller was ordering all aircraft passing over the Ice Cap to turn back immediately.

When Rayford asked for an explanation, all he received was a shouted warning: "All flights headed for North America over the Arctic Circle must turn back immediately. This is a matter of extreme urgency. It has come from the American Civil Defence headquarters in Washington, D.C. I repeat: Turn back! Do not attempt to land in North America!"

Unidentified aircraft had come like a swarm of bees from the north, over the Ice Cap and across Canada. With them had come missiles... hundreds (if not thousands) of them, flying high above the aircraft and coming down to earth just moments before the bombers crossed into U.S. airspace. Each missile had been programmed to hit a particular U.S. city or a strategic military target. Some were intercepted, of course, but on the whole the highly sophisticated American missile defence system had proved to be helpless in the face of so much fire-power and with so little warning.

The enemy missiles were each surrounded by a cluster of metallic balloons, which served to confuse tracking devices on the American anti-missile missiles. Nine out of ten of America's defence weapons totally missed their marks. And while American missiles were busily tracking other missiles, many of the enemy planes were able to sneak safely into U.S. airspace as well. What the missile invasion did not destroy, the enemy bombers took care of.

Although the general public had been conned into believing that America had an effective defence against an attack like this, military intelligence in almost every other country of the world knew better. But they also knew that nothing could stop America from pressing the button and sending its entire arsenal out to do the same thing to any other country that would dare to attack the U.S. By doing this, the United States could at least wipe their opponents out as they themselves were going down. This threat of "mutually assured destruction" (MAD, as it was called, for short) and *not* the highly touted missile defence system, had been the one thing that had kept the peace for as long as it had.

But now that the threat of nuclear attack had become a reality, the American system found itself either too unwieldy, too timid, or perhaps too sane to do to an enemy nation what was being done to itself. Someone in charge of pushing the button apparently realised, too late, that such a move would be pointless. It would not bring back to life the millions of Americans who died that night, and it would only double the suffering for the human race.

In Prospect Heights, Illinois, where Rayford Strait's family was sleeping, the air raid sirens went off several minutes before the first missiles hit, at 4am on Tuesday. But people had grown complacent about such things, ever since the Cold War had ended, and especially since communism had suffered such total defeat in the 1990's. The U.S. fallout shelter program was totally scrapped in 1992, and air raid drills were widely regarded as unnecessary, especially when they chose to go off in the middle of the night.

People in Prospect Heights, like people throughout the rest of the country, mostly rolled over in their beds, and either slept through the first impact or else never knew what hit them.

But Irene Strait was not like everyone else. She lived by the book, and if there was to be an air raid drill, then she would do the right thing by her country. She roused her family and they all trundled down to the basement, despite protests from both Chloe and Raymie.

On their way, Raymie grabbed what he thought was his latest hand-held video game lying on the kitchen counter. If he was going to be locked in the cellar for a while, he may as well have something to play with.

When they reached the basement, Irene turned on the transistor radio that she always kept there. She quickly picked up the special civil defence broadcast.

It was just dawning on the trio who sat huddled around the radio, that this was not a drill, when they heard and saw the first explosion. Downtown Chicago was some twenty miles south of them. When the first nuclear warhead hit it, they not only heard the explosion, but they also felt the rumble in the ground. The darkened basement lit up from the flash coming through two small street level windows. The windows themselves shook from the shock waves. A short while later, they heard several smaller explosions, with at least one of them coming from O'Hare International Airport, just six miles away, where a bomber had dropped a smaller bomb to destroy the runways.

The Strait family did not know it at the time, but one of those explosions came from a one megaton warhead that veered off course and landed between De Kalb and Dixon, some eighty miles west of them. It had been intended for a target just north of Prospect Heights. If it had landed as planned, their house would almost certainly have been destroyed, and if they had survived the blast, they would have been so badly burned from radiation that they would not have lived for more than a few days.

While they sat relatively safely in their basement, literally millions of Americans were being incinerated. Millions more were receiving burns and other injuries from which they would never recover.

"What's happening?" Irene said to herself in bewilderment, as she ran her hands through her hair.

"Are we being bombed?" asked Raymie. "It can't be the end of the world," he added, as if trying to reassure himself. "It can't be; we're s'posed ta be gone before that happens. It's not the end, is it, Mom?"

"I don't know, Raymie," Irene responded, with exasperation showing in her voice. "I've got to think."

"Quiet, you two," said Chloe, who had her ear pressed up against the radio. "They're saying that Russia has launched an attack. The missiles are from Russia. They say our defence system will stop the bombs before they reach their targets."

"Yeah, tell that to whoever just copped that last one!" said Raymie. "Bet it hit Chicago! Now we're gonna die too. We're gonna die; and what's God doing about it? He isn't doing anything, is he? Why, Mom? Why?" Raymie's voice was becoming more hysterical as the seriousness of the situation dawned on him.

"Settle down, Raymie! We need to pray," said Irene.

"Yeah, sure! We need to pray," he almost whispered sarcastically to himself. "We already *did* pray, and it was s'posed ta make us safe from all of this. I should be in heaven right now." He turned to Irene. "What went wrong, Mom? Why didn't we go? We're just as good as the others. How come they got raptured and we didn't?"

"We don't know that they *did* get raptured," said Raymie's mother. "Maybe the rapture hasn't happened yet."

"Well, what's the point, if we're still gonna hafta go through this?"

Chloe interrupted again. "Will both of you shut up? We're lucky to be alive right now. But it's not over yet. We need to act quickly."

Just then, the cellar lights went out.

"There should be some candles in that cupboard over the workbench," said Irene. "At least that's where we *used* to keep them."

Chloe felt her way over to the bench and opened the door on the overhanging cupboard. Not only were there candles, but there were matches too. She silently prayed that they would still light, and after a couple of strikes they had a reassuring flame perched on the workbench.

She turned to her younger brother. "Raymie, turn the faucet on and fill up the laundry tub with water. *Quickly*!" Chloe, like her father, was the pragmatist. She could see that decisions needed to be made, and she was making them. Her urgency jerked Raymie out of his wailing complaints, at least for a while.

Chloe turned to Irene. "Mom, stay by the radio and see if they tell us anything more. I need to find a way to cover those two windows as quickly as possible. There's a lot of radiation up there, and it's going to be around for quite a while."

Chloe found a hammer and some nails on an old work bench. She pulled boards off an orange crate and tacked them up in front of the two under-sized windows high up on the basement wall. There was still some coal in the corner of the old coal bin, and she stuffed as much of that as she could between the glass and the timber slats, in the hope that the coal would soak up some of the radiation. By the time she finished, she was covered with soot. But there was no time for cleaning up.

"Raymie, what's happening with the water?" Chloe asked.

"I filled the laundry tub and a bucket. There's nothing else to put it in."

"What about empty paint cans? Tip the paint out somewhere if you have to. We need to fill every available container, no matter how dirty it is."

Raymie went back to work looking for containers and muttering to himself about how no one would ever catch him drinking water from a dirty old paint can. "The paint's probably worse for me than not having any water at all," he said.

"There're only a couple dozen candles, and two boxes of matches," Chloe said, loudly enough for the others to hear. "We need to ration the candles *and* the water.

"What're we gonna eat?" asked Raymie.

"Nothing... at least not for a while. It's too dangerous to go upstairs. In a few days we may be able to make a quick trip to the fridge and grab something."

"In a few *days*?" wailed Raymie, who had tipped nails and screws out of some empty cans and was filling the cans with water.

"Yes, in a few days. It won't kill us."

Irene was not listening. She was fervently praying that God would do something to bring meaning to all of this. She prayed that he would protect them, that Rayford would be safe, and that she would be able to contact Pastor Billings. That was when she saw the cell phone.

Raymie had accidentally grabbed it, thinking it was a hand-held video game. She picked it up and started dialling. She thanked God that they had paid extra for the microwave satellite function. The Billingses had a satellite phone too. Hopefully she would be able to get a call through to them.

"Pastor Billings! Is that you?," she said when Vernon Billings picked up the receiver on his end of the line. "This is Irene Strait. What's happening? Please tell me!"

"Trust God, Sister Strait," said the kindly old pastor. "Everything's gonna be all right. He knows what he's doing."

"But the country... it's being bombed!" said Irene. "This isn't how it was supposed to happen. We were supposed to be *raptured*. Is this the end of the world or what?"

"Believe me, Sister. It's all under control" replied Pastor Billings. "I was on the phone to a Christian militia movement in Montana just last night. They said the Lord has actually *appeared* to them out there. Yes, really! It's not quite how we expected it to happen, but we have to flow with the Spirit, Sister. God is calling his people from all over America to make their way to Montana. I refused to believe it myself; but that was last night. Now I'm thinking differently."

There was silence on Irene's end of the phone as the pastor paused to let her respond. "Are you with me, Sister Strait?" he asked.

"Uh, yeah, sure. I'm with you," Irene replied hesitantly.

Pastor Billings continued. "We may escape this thing yet, Sister. But you'll have to be obedient. Elaine and I are praying about it now, and we want you to do the same. The Lord has spared us for a purpose. He's coming for us, Irene, you can be sure of that. We just had a few of the details wrong."

"A few of the *details*?!" said Chloe when Irene recounted her conversation a minute or two later. "The destruction of America is one hell of a big detail!"

"Watch your language," Irene cautioned. She should have known from past experience that such a warning would not stop her strong-willed daughter. Even bothering to make such a correction was out of character for Irene, who tended to let her children do what they liked.

"I'm sorry, Chloe," Irene said quickly. "It's all the pressure." And then she looked at her daughter in the light of the candle, with soot all over her face, and she longed once again for her to accept Jesus. Tears began to flow as she spoke, "This may be your last chance, honey. Wouldn't you like to get right with the Lord now, so that you can go with us?"

"I'm not going with *anyone* until I'm sure that it's safe out there," said Chloe. And then she added, "You aren't seriously thinking of going with him, are you? You'll get yourself killed!"

"What *else* are we supposed to do?" asked Raymie. "Just sit here and starve to death?"

Chloe shared her brother's frustration, but she did not let on. "What we need to do is sit here and listen to the radio. Civil Defence knows what's best. They said radiation is at its worst for the first 24 hours after the explosion. It could be suicidal to go out there now. Someone may come and rescue us. Or they may decide that it's safe for us to come out after a while. We just have to keep our heads and not panic. What they're saying now is for people to find shelter and wait."

Just then the phone rang. Irene picked it up. It was Rayford.

"Irene, I'm sorry to bother you at such an odd hour. I was worrying about you."

"Oh Rayford! It's awful! Chicago has been bombed, and some other cities too... No, *seriously*! It's on the radio... We're not hurt, just hiding in the basement... Are you okay? ... When will you be home? ... London? Why London? ... But you *will* be back tonight, won't you? ... Oh, this is awful! Just awful! ... Yes, I understand. ... I'll try. Do you have any idea how long you might be? ... I can't hear you. Your voice is breaking up... Oh dear, I've lost him."

Pan Continental, the airlines for which Rayford flew, had been the first to experiment with microwave satellite equipment on transatlantic flights. It was only good for a short, specified distance on each flight, but it meant that pilots had one more window through which to receive important information on long, lonely flights. Rayford had obviously used some of his precious satellite time to contact Irene.

Irene turned to the children. "Daddy couldn't land because of the bombs. He's on his way back to London. At least he's safe, and he knows we are too."

Zion Ben-Jonah Writes:

There is disagreement over whether Christians will be taken to heaven <u>before</u> the Great Tribulation, or <u>after</u>. Both sides agree: (1) That the seven 'trumpets' in chapters 8-10 of The Revelation refer to events that take place during the period called "The Great Tribulation"; and (2) That I Corinthians 15:51-52 is talking about what is called the Rapture -- when Christians will be caught up to meet Jesus in the air at his return. We need to study these passages to find the answer to the question about which comes first.

I Corinthians 15:51 says that the rapture will take place "at the sounding of the <u>last</u> trumpet". So when would that be? Before or after the seven trumpets of the Tribulation? Easy, isn't it?

Jesus himself says that "immediately <u>after</u> the tribulation of those days", God will send his angels to gather together those who believe in him, so that they can meet him as he returns to earth. (Matthew 24:29-31)

Teaching that Christians do not have to go through the Tribulation is popular, because it is what people <u>want</u> so badly to hear. But it is <u>not</u> supported by scripture. It is a false hope.

The real question in this debate is this: "What are the comparative risks involved in each approach?" Anyone bracing for the worst would not have a problem if proved wrong. But someone looking for an early escape would be in great despair if their theory proved unreliable.

2. Foretold

The control towers were in chaos, both at Gatwick and at Heathrow... in fact, all over Europe, as they tried to deal with so many returning flights. On his headphones in the cockpit of the big 747, Rayford Strait had been able to pick up something about a charter flight missing off the coast of Scotland. It had run out of fuel while trying to get back to England. There was no telling what had become of the many flights which would not have had enough fuel to make it back to Europe. They would have been forced to put down somewhere in North America, with or without airport runways. There must have been dozens of crashes.

When Rayford had landed and walked into the airport, he started to get a clearer picture of the enormity of the problem. Amidst the pandemonium of flight cancellations and unscheduled arrivals the airport was abuzz with talk about a huge pre-emptive military strike against the United States, by Russia. It was 2pm in London, but only 8am in Chicago. The sun had not even come up on the West Coast of America yet, and it would be a few hours before any video coverage would be available, but every news station in the world was interrupting its normal programming to give sketchy first reports of the disaster.

Early estimates put the deaths at five million. Later reports would verify that the loss in human life was already several times that figure, and it would almost double over the next few weeks.

Damage to cities, highways, and airports meant that reconstruction was out of the question... even if there had been no nuclear fallout to worry about. The entire country was without government, without power, without communication, and without vital transportation links. The central business district of nearly a hundred major American cities had been entirely wiped out. If the attack had not come in the middle of the night, the loss in human lives would have been several times higher.

Hospitals in the inner cities had been destroyed, and along with them had gone their entire on-duty medical staffs. What medical and rescue services were still available had to function almost without administration, and that was assuming that the rescue personnel themselves were still alive and able to work. America was suddenly back in the middle ages; everyone was being forced to fend for themselves to survive.

Emergency services throughout the English-speaking world were quick to start marshalling forces to airlift rescue supplies, protective clothing, and medical personnel to America, Mexico, and Canada. The wounded would need to be treated as quickly as possible, although for many hundreds of thousands, even treatment would not save them. Those who were already dead would most likely be left where they were.

There were mixed feelings from the non-English-speaking world. Everyone was, of course, shocked. But U.S. President Gerald Fitzhugh had made many enemies with his growing military involvement in world affairs. Or perhaps it was because of his *non*-involvement. Whereas he had been quick to volunteer troops to wipe out anyone he regarded as *terrorists*, he had been turning a blind eye to the growing number of right-wing military dictatorships that were spreading around the globe, especially those in Africa and South America.

Xu Dangchao, from Tibet, had been elected Secretary General of the United Nations one year earlier, two years after Tibet had been admitted to the world body. Although his policies were wildly popular with the Third World, his hands had been tied because of America's veto power in the U.N. Security Council. Dangchao wanted to erase the Third World debt and to do away with prejudicial import/export duties, which had the effect of favouring rich nations and further crippling the poorer ones. America's weak justification for opposing the scheme was just that Dangchao was trying to do "too much too soon".

Dangchao was backed by Russia and China, who were as stubborn as America about vetoing *American* proposals for military intervention in countries where basic human rights were being abused. Of course, the U.S. had other avenues, and other treaties (like the old NATO alliance), that it could call on when ways were needed to circumvent a veto from either Russia or China.

Sadly, President Fitzhugh found that the more he had played God with the future of other countries, the easier it had become to justify interference even when the civil rights abuses by the side he was helping were worse than those by the ones he was committing America to destroy.

Of course the American public had lapped it all up. The important thing, politically, was that Fitzhugh had not lost a single skirmish while he had been in office. As long as he was careful to target small revolutionary movements and to hit them hard and hit them without warning, he was almost guaranteed success. Troops would no sooner return triumphant from one conflict than he would be sending out more to settle another dispute. Americans were more proud than ever to be Americans. They truly saw themselves as the saviours of the world. And President Fitzhugh, with his claim to being born again, never missed an opportunity to enlist God in his campaigns, and to remind the voters that God was on his side.

But now, with America in the throes of death, Russia and China had nothing to fear either from Fitzhugh, or from Britain or France -- the other two permanent members of the Security Council. It appeared that all three of the dissenting nations had been well and truly subdued in the space of just a few hours!

* * *

Rayford was told to get some sleep, but to stay in touch with the airport, so that he could be called in if his plane was needed for a mercy mission. All commercial flights to the U.S. had been cancelled. The British government had already declared a state of emergency. This meant that the British military would take command of all local airlines and all local airline pilots. Australia, New Zealand, South Africa, and many European nations were making similar moves to assist. Supplies urgently needed to be flown to North America, and refugees needed to be flown out. The entire population of the U. S. was about to be evacuated ... at least what remained of it.

There had been no reports of damage in Canada, apart from a couple of hits in unpopulated regions, and these were apparently caused by defective missiles. It seemed that Russia's war was only with the U.S., and not with Canada.

England, Australia, and other countries that were sympathetic with America had also escaped without a hint of attack. So airports in Toronto, Ottawa, Montreal, Quebec, and Vancouver were being geared up for round the clock arrivals and departures. Rayford, along with all other available pilots, would be playing an important part in the rescue operation.

Although he was tired from the trip, there was too much happening for Rayford to sleep straight away. He checked into the Airport Hilton, then laid on the bed fully clothed. He stared at the ceiling and thought deeply. He thought about Irene and about Chloe and about Raymie. His concerns turned only briefly to other relatives in the U.S. who might have been hit. Telephone communication with the United States was virtually impossible because so many lines had been knocked out. Even satellite phones were being affected by the fallout. Rayford had bought Irene one of the new microwave satphones, so that he could call her from the cockpit when passing through the relatively narrow band on the Pan-Con route from London to Chicago. That would now be his main link with her. He would probably be able to give her another call on his flight back to Canada.

Rayford thought of how it must have been for the millions who had already died. Then he thought of Irene and the children down in the basement. There was comfort in knowing that they were still alive. With any luck, he would be talking to them again within the next 24 hours. He took a moment to thank God for that. In time, he hoped to be able to find a way to get rescuers to the house, so they could take his family to safety.

Late in the afternoon, after a few hours of fitful sleep, Rayford awoke, showered, and then left word at the hotel desk that he was catching a cab to the airport. He figured that airline officials could tell him more about what was happening than he would be able to learn from any other news source.

A visit to the airline offices above the departure lounge revealed that Rayford had been assigned to fly out at six the next morning, on a flight to Toronto. There would be only a few passengers, but the plane would also carry tents, medical supplies, food, and radiation-proof clothing. They were already being loaded in a special hangar at the south end of the airport.

Rayford further learned that, when word had begun to spread, only hours after the bombing had stopped, that Canada had not been hit, this had started a mass northern exodus from the United States. The northern highways were already packed with people fleeing the scene. Canadian authorities were frantically trying to set up refugee camps to contain them.

Fortunately, it was nearly summer, so thousands of people were quickly accommodated outside, near Canada's border with the U.S. This left churches and school auditoriums free to be turned into hospitals for the wounded. Helicopters and land rescue vehicles started almost immediately to ferry the wounded out of the northern states; but even then they were only able to service a few of the worst hit cities. Vancouver was caring for the wounded from Seattle, Portland, and Spokane; Toronto was taking survivors from Detroit, Cleveland, and Buffalo; and Ottawa, Montreal and Quebec were doing what they could to help refugees from the area that included Boston, Rochester, Philadelphia, and New York City.

At the same time, Canadians themselves were panicking about the fallout that was headed their way. Airports in all of the major cities were packed with passengers waiting for stand-by seats out of the country. Hundreds of flights which would have normally been destined for the U.S. were quickly rerouted to Canada, where airlines could be guaranteed to fill every seat, regardless of what they charged or where their destination was to be. Officials from Emergency Preparedness Canada were frantically trying to set up priority criteria for determining who should be allowed to take the first flights out of the country.

A TV in the Heathrow VIP lounge updated viewers on how many U.S. cities and airports had been demolished. Aircraft were still able to come and go from some smaller airstrips. But that would not be enough to meet the far more urgent needs of the larger cities -- cities like Chicago -- which were the ones that had suffered the greatest losses. Milwaukee and St. Paul/Minneapolis, both closer to Canada than Chicago, were on their own in providing transport to the refugee camps being set up by their northern neighbours.

President Gerald Fitzhugh and his family were believed to be trapped beneath the capital building in Washington, D.C., where they had been rushed to shelter as soon as the alert went up. If a bomb had landed close enough to bring down the White House (which appeared to be the case), then escape for those beneath it would not be easy.

People who had survived the bombing were being told via radio broadcasts to seek shelter and to await further instructions. There would be attempts to relocate them to places away from the fallout; but first the authorities needed to establish exactly where that might be. Weather reports before the attack showed a cold front moving southeast across the Midwest. The fallout cloud would, therefore, be likely to move in that direction. However this was only good news for people on the American West Coast, because for every cloud moving away from other localities, there was another coming toward them from the west.

With nuclear strikes in San Diego, Anaheim, L.A., Fresno, Sacramento, Oakland, San Francisco, Portland, Eugene, Tacoma, Seattle, and Spokane, states on the West Coast were amongst the most heavily hit anyway. Only the area between Boston and Washington had been more heavily hit.

Rayford could see from the first film footage of refugees heading for Canada, that he and his family would not have much chance of reunion through that route. Both sides of the freeways were being used for northbound traffic, which was at a standstill in places and only creeping along in others. Traffic had to detour around major cities and other badly damaged roads. Against such a flow of traffic, only emergency vehicles had any hope of travelling south.

The freeways themselves were becoming increasingly blocked by vehicles without fuel, which had to be pushed to the side of the road and deserted. That left the drivers and passengers of those vehicles to venture forward on foot. Days out on the road would mean days more exposed to the deadly fallout. Civil Defence warned against trying to escape before it could be established that there was someplace safe to go. But millions took no heed.

Chicago was too far away from Toronto to attract Toronto's limited rescue resources. But some local authorities in the Chicago area were commandeering aircraft, vehicles, and even ships to ferry survivors north. Everyone working on rescue operations was putting themselves at risk, and protective clothing was urgently required.

Rayford took some consolation in knowing that, even if he could not get to his own family, he would be helping the overall rescue effort. In time his involvement might give him the opening that he needed to help Irene and the kids as well.

Rayford left the VIP lounge at about 7pm and headed for the cab rank. He had learned as much as he could, and now it was time to get a few more hours of sleep before his departure. On the way out of the airport lobby, he was approached by a slim, blond man, in his thirties. The shabbily dressed man stuck a booklet in Rayford's face and asked in a broad German accent if he wanted to read it. *The Fall of America* was the title. It appeared above a picture of an upside-down American flag. Rayford pushed the man aside in disgust.

Always someone ready to cash in on the sufferings of others! he thought to himself. But just as he walked out the door of the airport, it hit him: The attack had only taken place a few hours ago! How could someone in England already have produced a booklet telling about it? He raced back into the airport, his eyes searching in every direction for the man. The little German was near the Pan-Con ticket counter, talking to two or three other people, who also appeared to be sending him away.

"Where did you get that? Who wrote it?" Rayford whispered almost at the level of a shout, when he had caught the man's attention by grabbing his arm. He was trying hard not to create a scene, and yet he was desperate to know what was going on.

"Some friends... together, vee wrote it," the man replied, half in fear. "You are interested?" he asked.

"Yes, I'm interested!" said Rayford emphatically. "*Very* interested. But first tell me how you knew it was going to happen."

"Vee study Bible prophecy," said the softly-spoken little man. "And vee pray. Vee have been saying dat dis vould happen. Vee have been saying it for a few years now. It is most imperative dat you read dis book." His brow was wrinkled in an almost exaggerated show of seriousness. But then, how could anyone possibly exaggerate the seriousness of what had just happened in America?

The young German went on dramatically: "Udder sings are coming too... Ferry *serious* sings."

Rayford wanted to read the book; but he also wanted some instant answers. He offered the man -- Reinhard was his name -- a meal, if he would sit down and talk to him.

"It is most important dat I get dese books to da people," replied Reinhard. "Vee can talk later."

"Please!" Rayford begged, almost in tears now. "I'll be flying to Canada tonight. My family is over there. I must know what is going on before I leave."

Reinhard sensed an urgency in Rayford's voice that he must not have found in his other clients, because he quickly backed down. "Vere do you vant to talk?" he asked.

Rayford took him to a table in the nearest restaurant, ordered a meal for them both and then opened the floor for Reinhard to explain what was going on.

"Vat is happening now... it is yudgement from God on America. But it is also opening for Russia to control da United Nations. You understand?" Rayford knew of the growing unrest throughout the world at what many countries considered was America's abuse of power within the U. N. That much of Reinhard's explanation made sense, but it was not what he was looking for.

"Are you telling me that you knew this was going to happen just from reading the Bible?" he asked incredulously.

"I cannot show all vat you vish to know in such short time. You vill read it in the book." In his clipped German manner, Reinhard's promise sounded more like a command. "You vill see for yourself. For now, vee have little time. I must move quickly. The Bible tells of five vorld powers. They are a bear, an eagle, a lion, a leopard, and a rooster. Dese are signs for Russia, America, England, Africa, and France." He counted them off on his fingers. "You must know, dee leopard is being now used as sign of solidarity for da Tird Vorld."

Rayford was finding it difficult to follow, but he decided to let Reinhard carry on.

"England, France, and America can veto plans by Russia and China in dee United Nations. Dee udder ten Security Council members... dey are called *rotating* members... Dey come from dee udder countries."

"So?" said Rayford, who was showing only mild interest at this stage. He had other questions that he wanted to ask, but he would wait a bit longer.

Reinhard went on. "Dee eagle's vings are plucked. You vill see it in the book. It is in the Bible. Dis bombing, it is dee plucking of dee eagle's vings. After falls dee eagle, da lion... dat is, England... loses its power. Da rooster vings, dey join vit da leopard. Dat is France and all of Europe joining vit da Tird Vorld. You see, it is because da bear... Russia... *subdues*... Dat is to say she *stops* three vorld powers from fighting against her. She does it by plucking da vings of da eagle. Vit help from dee udder ten nations da new leader vill control da vorld."

Rayford was losing patience. "I'm not interested in all the political stuff," he said. "Do you have any answers? My family is over there. If you really know what is going on, what can I do for them? What *should* I do?"

"It is God's punishment," Reinhard said soberly. "If dey are alive, dey vill be forced to leave. No one vill live dere *ever again*. God is angry vit the shurch people in America."

"The church people?" Rayford said with genuine surprise. "Why the church people?" He was thinking of Irene.

"Dey fight da teachings of sheesus. Dey do not prepare for vat is coming, and dey do not tell the truth to udders."

"My *wife* is a church person," Rayford responded indignantly. "She was *always* talking about this... this... something called The Great Tribulation."

"No, no! Dis is not da Great Tribulation... yet," said Reinhard. Dis is only da *start* of vat is coming. But your vife she needs faith dat is strong enough to go *through* da Great Tribulation. I do not sink she vill find it in the shurches."

"She doesn't *need* to go through it... least not the way *she* tells it," Rayford replied. He was surprised to hear himself defending something he had always scoffed at. "She says that she will be taken to heaven before it happens."

"And did she tell you dat America vas going to be punished before she goes to heffen?" Reinhard asked quietly, as he stared at his lap. When Rayford did not answer immediately, Reinhard raised his head, and then his blond eyebrows in further anticipation.

Rayford finally spoke. "Well, I don't know. I don't recall her saying anything about that." Even as he spoke, he was thinking about how emotional Irene had been on the phone. "Maybe she missed that part."

"She vill need help ... *spiritual* help." Reinhard said sympathetically. He went on slowly, as though talking to himself: "It is so ferry hard for the shurch people... Dey cannot say ven dey are wrong." Then he looked Rayford directly in the eyes, and spoke slowly and deliberately, his own eyes opening wide as he spoke. "You must not let her run avay. She vill vant to run off and find her Sheesus."

Rayford did not like hearing his wife talked about in such a way at a time when he was so close to losing her. He would take the time to study Reinhard's book more closely later, but he was not getting any information from this strange little man that would help him in his present situation. So he excused himself and left Reinhard to finish his meal alone.

Rayford wondered as he glanced back at the skinny little street preacher wolfing the last of the food down, just how long it had been since Reinhard's last meal.

Zion Ben-Jonah Writes:

Predictions about the fall of America are mostly based on Daniel 7:1-7 and Revelation 13:1-2. Daniel's prophecy is usually assumed to be about the original Babylonian Empire (represented by a Lion with Eagle wings), the Persian Empire (represented by a Bear), the Greek Empire (represented by a Leopard with four chicken wings), and the Roman Empire (represented by a horrible 'Beast' that devours the whole earth). And yet these same symbols apply to four of the five members of the U.N. Security Council. (The symbol for the fifth member, China, is a Dragon.) Only the leopard (or panther) is not a prominent national symbol today, except as a symbol for Africa, militant Blacks, or, perhaps, the Third World.

In Revelation 13:2, a _future_ world power is described which has attributes of all the animals listed in Daniel 7, _except_ the Eagle. The Eagle, apparently, no longer exists at that time!

There are ten rotating members of the U.N. Security Council, taken from the rest of the world. The Bible says that with the help of ten "kings" a resurrected world power will destroy another world power described as a Prostitute... who rules over world trade. (Revevelation 17:1-5, 12-16) And her name is Babylon.

The _Encyclopedia Britannica_ lists only one city in the modern world which is named Babylon. It is located on Long Island, in New York City, not far from the New York Stock Exchange!

3. Lo Here and Lo There!

When the sun was up, enough light filtered into the basement of the Strait's house in Prospect Heights, to enable the three prisoners to find their way around without the use of a candle.

Chloe designated one corner of the basement as the latrine. Water was no longer flowing through the pipes, so she urged everyone to drink their fill of water from one of the smaller containers, and then instructed them to use that to catch their urine. They would do that with all of the containers as the water supply dwindled.

"We may have to recycle it if we run out of water," Chloe explained.

"Gross!" said Raymie. "Like why don't we just get water from upstairs?"

"One problem," said Chloe. "There *is* none. Pipes have probably broken somewhere closer to where the bomb hit. We may be able to get something from the refrigerator in a few days; but even that won't be much more than a water bottle and some ice cube trays. I'm not saying that we would actually drink our own urine; but we have to be prepared, just in case."

Chloe found some old newspapers and put them in one corner, along with some cardboard boxes to catch bowel movements.

"And what are we going to do about the smell?" asked Raymie.

"One of two things," said Chloe, who was beginning to lose patience with her younger brother. "Either we put up with it or we bellyache. And we already know which you will do."

Irene remained silent and deep in thought. She was facing a difficult decision.

Then, at 9am, according to Chloe's watch, some five hours after the bombs had landed, the trio looked up as one when they heard footsteps running across the floor above them. The basement door flew open and Vernon and Elaine Billings came tripping down the steps. Light from the house above was blinding to those who had become accustomed to manoeuvring in the dark, and the darkness below was equally blinding to Vernon and Elaine.

"Quickly! Close the door!" shouted Chloe. Elaine Billings promptly shut the door, and then reached out for her husband's shoulder as she stumbled in the darkness. Vernon Billings was a big man, and he had no difficulty holding up his much smaller wife.

"My, it certainly is dark down here!" Pastor Billings remarked, as he held tightly to the railing. "Don't you have any candles?"

"We do, but we're conserving them," Chloe said coldly. She knew that she should be more polite to the minister and his wife. They were always sweet and polite to her. And yet something about them rubbed her the wrong way.

"Sister Strait, you must hear what has happened!" exclaimed Vernon Billings. "Go ahead! Tell them Elaine!"

Elaine Billings obediently responded. "You see, Irene, we prayed about this business in Montana, after Vern talked to you on the phone this morning. We asked God to give us a sign if this really was him.

"We were both sitting there in the cellar, having breakfast when it happened. Vern heard this voice. Well, we both did," she said, with a nervous look toward her husband. "And it said 'Come!' Just like that: 'Come!' "

Pastor Billings picked up the story from there. "We talked about it for a while, and then Elaine went up to the kitchen and brought down her promise box. We pulled out a card and it was the one from the end of Mark's Gospel, where it says, 'If you eat any deadly thing, it will not hurt you.'

"Can you see what God was saying, Sister? He was giving us a promise that he would protect us if we would just head out for Montana right now. We've packed up food, water, and a few clothes, and we're ready to go.

"But we want to give you a chance to come too. Are you with us, Sister?"

Elaine piped in sweetly, "Please come with us, Irene."

"Oh, I don't know," Irene answered. "Are you sure it's safe? Wouldn't it be better to wait a little while first?"

"And miss out on the rapture?" asked Elaine. "Look, we've been out there in the open for at least half an hour now, and we're as good as gold.

I was scared at first too, but I'm not now."

"God'll protect you, Irene." Pastor Billings said softly. "I'm sure of it. Please, trust him, and come with us, Irene!"

"Can we, Mom?" asked Raymie. "It's better than staying in here. Look, it hasn't hurt *them*!"

"What about *you*, Chloe? Will you come with us?" Irene asked, the pained expression on her face pleading desperately with her daughter.

"No way! If you want to do something stupid like that, I... I don't want to be a part of it. Seriously, Mom, do you think this is the way God would do it? I think you're all panicking because things didn't turn out the way you expected. Just admit that you were wrong. It's no big deal!"

"I come against this doubting spirit!" Pastor Billings said as his eyes narrowed and he lifted his hand toward Chloe. The big man looked even bigger as he stood a few steps from the bottom of the stairs in the semidarkness. Chloe recoiled in shock. She had never seen this side of the man before, and she did not like it at all.

"I rebuke you doubting spirit, in *Jesus*' name!" he shouted dramatically.

And then Pastor Billings lowered his hand and resumed his saccharin voice. "The car's waiting, Sister," he said softly. "It's *your* choice now. You can step out in faith or you can stay here and miss the rapture. What will it be, Dear? It's time to leave." And he started to move back up the steps.

"Please, Chloe!" said Irene pathetically. "Please come with us!" as she too moved toward the door.

"Mom, no! You don't know what you're doing!" Chloe shouted, shocked that her mother was so quick to believe two people who had talked themselves into believing what they, too, badly wanted to believe. "What about Daddy?"

"Tell him that I love him," was all that Irene could get out before she turned and raced, sobbing, up the steps. Elaine and Vernon had already reopened the door and stepped out into the hallway near the kitchen.

"Are you coming, Raymie?" Irene said almost as an afterthought. She had naturally assumed that young Raymie would go along with whatever she decided.

"Bye, Sis," Raymie said, with a one-armed hug. "Sorry for all the bad times I gave you." And he too headed up the steps.

Chloe was too shocked to answer. Raymie was at the top of the stairs before she could say a word, and then all she said was, "Raymie... No..."

And they were gone.

Zion Ben-Jonah Writes

The description of the situation on earth prior to the return of Jesus is one of people panicking because he has not turned up at the time when they had been expecting him to come. Jesus warns, in Matthew 24: "If they should say to you, 'Lo here, or Lo there!' go not after them. If they say that he is in the desert', do not go after them. Or if they say that he is in a secret place, do not believe it. For as the lightning is seen from the East to the West, even so will the coming of the Son of Man be." (verses 23-27)

So much for any "secret rapture"!

The real source of the secret rapture doctrine and a lot of other teachings in the church world today is one of escapism. It is so easy to deceive ourselves into believing what we <u>want</u> to believe, whether or not it is true. It could be a teaching that we will never be sick, or that we will be prosperous, or that we can go on disobeying Jesus and God will overlook it, or that we will not have to go through the Tribulation. All such teachings are popular, not because they are true, but because they are so appealing. They say what people want to hear.

Unless Christians are able to acknowledge error when it is pointed out (through circumstances if nothing else), they will only replace one form of escapism with an even more bizarre form, in an effort to further escape facing their error.

4. Searching

When he was back at the Hilton, Rayford opened the booklet. He noted on the back cover that Reinhard and his friends called themselves Jesans. He then turned to the book's introduction:

We all find it easier to see faults in others than it is to see them in ourselves. The people of America are no exception. When you observe all the religious activity in the United States today, it is easy to see how people (both in and out of the churches) have been fooled into confusing religion with real faith. But religious activities, rituals, even emotional experiences have little to do with good old-fashioned obedience to the things that Jesus taught in the Bible. And America's disobedience will be punished before anyone else's, because those who know the most have the most to answer for.

The introduction went on...

*If it is any consolation, the Bible promises that there will be an even bigger day of reckoning for the rest of the world than that which will fall on the United States of America. But the Bible also says that judgment must **begin** with those who claim to be God's people. (I Peter 4:17) And as we will elaborate on in this booklet, the judgment of America is going to make the destruction of Sodom and Gomorrah sound like a Sunday School picnic.*

"Well, that much is true," thought Rayford Strait. He then read on:

It just happens that God often used a conven-
ient heathen nation to judge his people--Israel.
Because America is the New Testament equivalent of Israel, God will use atheistic communism
to carry out his judgment on America. No big
deal. It's not a spiritual competition between
America and any other political power. It's just a
matter of personal accountability on the part of
those who should know better.

Billy Graham is reported to have once said, "If
God doesn't destroy America, he owes Sodom
and Gomorrah an apology." The assumption, of
course, is that God should destroy America because of its homosexuality, or its atheism, or its
prostitution, or gambling, or drugs, or abortions.
But presumably **not** because of the sins of the
churches: materialism, pride, hypocrisy, self-righteousness, or any of the other things that Jesus
actually got cranked up about.

Abraham assumed that there were at least 100
righteous people in Sodom in his day. He probably
did so because many of them attended his synagogue or supported his evangelistic crusades. But
God knew otherwise. Abraham had been deceived
by religious double-talk. When Jesus compared the
sins of Sodom to the sins of our day, he made no
mention of homosexuality, witchcraft, or any of the
sensational stuff. He just said the problem was
materialism and family commitments, even amongst
those who attended the synagogue (or whatever
the "churches" were called in those days).

It was about this stage that Rayford lost interest. He had maintained peace in his marriage through an unspoken truce with Irene: He would tolerate her church involvement if she would tolerate his *non*-involvement. At times he had consented to attend church in exchange for favours from her; but what the Jesans were suggesting was that he should get religion *and* alienate himself from Irene at the same time. What a lose/lose situation!

He tossed the book into his travel bag and went to sleep.

At 5am Rayford returned to the airport to fly the 6am mercy flight to Toronto. A few hours out of London, he entered the satphone communication band. Unfortunately, most of that precious time was taken up with official information coming from airport control in Toronto.

As it happened, Rayford had made a short list of what needed to be said to Irene, so that he could make the best use of the few seconds that remained of satphone time, when the official business had been completed. Although it was after 3am in Illinois, Chloe answered on the second ring. That was fortunate, thought Rayford. Chloe was a clearer thinker than Irene, and she would follow his instructions well.

"Chloe, this is Dad. I only have one minute, so listen closely. Do you have a pencil and paper handy?"

"Yes, Dad, but..."

"Good. Please turn the phone off for 48 hours after I hang up, so the battery will last longer. Got it?"

Chloe had already thought of that, and she had left the phone turned off for much of the previous day, since she knew her father could not have made another call for at least 18 hours. Although she badly wanted to share her news, she was still taking notes as she had been told to do. "Yes, I've got that. But, Dad..."

"I'll be in Toronto by 8:30 your time, and I'll make sure that the rescue people there know about you. I'll phone with more details on my way back to London in a couple of days."

"Dad!" Chloe shouted. "Mom's gone!"

"Gone? Gone where?" Rayford assumed that Irene had gone out to get some provisions, forgetting that it was three in the morning in Prospect Heights.

"I don't know! Somewhere in Montana. She went with Vernon and Elaine Billings yesterday. They think *Jesus* is out there. Raymie went with them. I *tried* to stop them, Dad. I *tried!*""

Although deeply shocked, it took only a moment for Rayford to conclude that his primary duty lay with rescuing Chloe now. Only a few seconds remained in the satphone link.

"Okay. We'll deal with that later," he said. "But for now, what's *your* situation, honey?"

Chloe, too, must have made a mental list of things to say. This was her chance to use it.

"I'm fine, Dad. Water is a bigger concern than food at the moment, but there's no urgent need. So far I'm feeling fine, just a bit tired."

He was getting more static than information now. Their window of communication was coming to an end.

"You're doing great, honey! I love you!" Rayford shouted, not knowing whether she heard any of it.

Then his thoughts returned to the shocker. Irene. Run off to Montana to find Jesus? Surely his wife was more sane than that! What could she have been thinking? Then he remembered Reinhard's expression of concern about Irene doing just that. How could this total stranger have known that she would behave so out of character? He had asked Reinhard for some *practical* advice, but then he had missed it when it was offered. How embarrassing!

The plane was on automatic, so Rayford turned to his first officer. "Can you watch things for an hour or so, Chris?" he asked.

The co-pilot squinted as he looked out the window to the path ahead of them. "Roger," he replied dutifully. "No problem."

Rayford fished the book which he had dismissed so casually a few hours earlier, out of his travel bag.

By the time they reached Canada, he had a much better understanding of what the Jesans were saying.

They had predicted a Russian missile attack over the North Pole. They had also prophesied that all survivors would be evacuated from America, and that the entire country would be abandoned because of fallout and because of the extent of the damage.

The recent rise in new diseases, an increase in the number and intensity of earthquakes, and spreading danger from destruction of the ozone layer were also referenced from Bible prophecy.

Other predictions had not yet taken place, and those interested Rayford even more. He made a mental note of each of them. In particular, he was struck by what the book had to say about changes in the United Nations. From the news broadcasts it appeared that Russia's war with America had ended as quickly as it had started. Russia had even come forward with offers to assist in the American aid and evacuation operation. Secretary General Dangchao had held a press conference only hours after the news broke, in which he assumed responsibility for coordinating the relief effort. The whole attack was being treated more like a natural disaster than a war for which Russia was totally responsible.

It intrigued Rayford that the Jesans' little book could have so accurately predicted it all. The book explained how America's greed had actually *created* much of the world's poverty. The brain drain, monopolies on information technology, multinational investment strategies in the

Third World, and the transformation of limited Third World farmland into luxury crops like tea, rubber, coffee, cotton, sugar, tobacco, spices, and fast-growing timber forests all depleted the Third World of badly needed labour, technology, and resources for their own development. Unbelievable waste in America came at the expense of the rest of the world. Even U.S. aid was calculated to enhance American power, through loans and military aid. At best American aid was like offering a band-aid to someone whom they had just tortured to death.

Rayford considered arguing with all that he read; but by the time that he had finished reading, he was beginning to doubt a few of his own arguments.

* * *

It had been a little over 24 hours since the first missiles had hit. Already hundreds of thousands of refugees were pouring into Canada from the U.S. Few of the first arrivals were seriously injured, but most were showing early signs of radiation sickness: nausea, tiredness, loss of appetite. For some this would develop into dangerous infections, destruction of intestinal linings, brain damage, and even death. This was the price they would pay for having exposed themselves so soon after the bombs went off.

The whole of Toronto (like other Canadian cities) was being pushed into action to accommodate their southern neighbours. It seemed already that things were out of control, and the real rush had barely begun. Over six million people would be processed through the city of Toronto alone over the next two months.

Rayford spent the next two days going from one agency to another looking for help for Chloe. He would telephone first, but whenever he found someone who might be hopeful, he would catch a cab and turn up in person, hoping to make himself known to some official who could give him favoured treatment when an opportunity arose to reach Chloe. Along the way, he donated a pint of blood, and put in a couple of hours constructing tents at a football field on the south side of the city. His interest was not totally selfish. He genuinely wanted to help.

In the end he had to settle for supplying particulars on Chloe, Irene, Raymie, and the Billingses to a growing international register, which would be used to determine the number of fatalities, and to link up loved ones as survivors turned up.

The Pan Con schedule called for Rayford to return to London on Friday evening. It was against normal regulations for him to be making a third flight in so few days; but personally, he would have been happy to leave earlier. In terms of reaching Chloe, he was almost as helpless in Toronto as he had been in London. But each flight meant one more call to Chloe... at least until the phone battery went dead.

Although Chloe, Raymie, and Irene were his main concern, Rayford had also been thinking about what Reinhard had said, and about his own relationship with God. He had always believed in God, even though he rarely mentioned it. In a crisis he would instinctively ask for help from God. Although his arguments against the church were mostly excuses for his own indifference to spiritual matters, he fully believed that real faith required something more than what he saw in the churches.

Now it looked like he may have found it. Churchy efforts to convert him had been an irritation; but the Jesans' very *existence* was far more irritating. Here were people who apparently had the goods. They could see through the shallowness of religion--including American evangelicalism--and they were offering a real alternative. He was bothered by what he heard, but at the same time, he needed to know more.

So on Friday morning, Rayford called the cell phone number that Reinhard had given him, to see if he could arrange a meeting with the Jesans when he had returned to London.

"Vee will be distributing in Hounslow on Saturday, and spending tomorrow night at Heston services, on the M-4," Reinhard said.

"Don't you have an office?" Rayford asked.

"No, ve yust have a friend's garage, vere vee keep our tracts," Reinhard answered.

"But where do you sleep?"

"In da van. You vill see tomorrow," Reinhard promised.

Zion Ben-Jonah Writes

There are many prophecies that warn of a surprise military attack on Israel "from the north". A number of Bible expositors have seen Russia as the one making the attack. However, most overlooked the fact that the <u>United States</u> is the modern day equivalent of Israel, and that an attack on the U.S. by Russia from over the North Pole would <u>also</u> be "from the north".

In the opening chapter of the book of Jeremiah, God asks the prophet what he is looking at one night, and he says that he is looking at a pot of boiling water. He says, "The face thereof is toward the north." God goes on to tell him that the pot symbolises trouble that is coming from the north... trouble that will put his people in "hot water" figuratively speaking. (Jeremiah 1:13--14)

It is interesting that the most significant constellation in the Northern Hemisphere is the Big Dipper (or 'big pot'), and that you need only line up the two stars on the "face" of it to locate the North Star. The North Star is the most significant star in yet another constellation... the constellation called in Latin, Ursa (or Russia)... the Bear!

5. On the Road to Montana

It was nearing nine o'clock on a cool Friday evening in May. The scene was a remote highway interchange in the far north of the American Midwest. At any other time in history, it may have been a night to reflect on the beauties of creation. But in the midst of the greatest destruction the world had ever known, this was no place for such grand thoughts.

Irene Strait looked across the campfire at the older man. She had feelings of pity for him, but they were mixed with feelings of disillusionment that bordered on revulsion. For years she had respected him--maybe even idolised him. She had often wished that her own husband could be more like him. Even now Vernon Billings showed outstanding strength and determination. His obsession with reaching Montana continued to drive him on, even though it was looking more and more like he would eventually die from the effects of his foolhardy decision.

It would not be fair to call Vernon Billings a con man, for if he was, he had conned himself as well. He had offered to sleep out on the ground that first night, outside of Eau Claire, Minnesota, so that Raymie and the women could sleep more comfortably inside the car. Only when it had started to rain and he had become drenched, had he sought refuge with them inside the vehicle. Fallout from the bombing in Minneapolis was already on the ground, and more came down with the rain.

Vernon slept out again on Thursday night, just inside the North Dakota state border, on Highway 94. All of this exposure had made his prognosis much worse than that of most of the other pilgrims camped inside the cloverleaf on the intersection between Highway 94, going west, and Highway 85, going north to Regina, Canada.

But Irene was not thinking about what had motivated Vernon to camp out on the first two nights, whether it was heroism or stupidity. What she was thinking about was his behaviour that same day.

Food and water were scarce and expensive; but gasoline was the biggest concern for millions of travellers on the nation's highways. Tankers were no longer operating, so stations that sold at normal prices had quickly exhausted their stocks. Traffic was bumper to bumper in places, and often stop and go, as cars sought ways around damaged sections of the highway and around abandoned cars. This slowed progress and increased fuel consumption as well.

By Friday morning, any stations that still had fuel could name their own price. Checks and credit cards were useless, and it was not possible to get funds from the banks. The Prospect Heights pilgrims had less than $100 left when they had pulled into a station just before noon, advertising gas for $1,000 a tank. The situation was desperate.

Vernon Billings stopped the big Lincoln Town Car next to the pumps and leaned his head on the steering wheel for a moment while he prayed. He then lifted his head, leaned over Elaine to pull a cloth bag from the glove box, and turned to Irene in the back seat. "Irene, can you put the nozzle in the tank and start pumping when the attendant turns it on?" Irene caught a look of horror on Elaine's face.

"No, Vern. Don't...." Elaine began.

"I'll leave the motor running to save time," Vernon said, ignoring Elaine as he headed for the gas station store. He stayed inside while Irene filled up. When she had replaced the gas hose, Vernon ran out, hopped into the driver's seat and squealed the tyres as he tore out of the driveway.

No one said anything, but they all knew that he had used the gun in the cloth bag to get the gas.

"It's not like I robbed it," he said, as Elaine glared at him from the passenger seat. "I left him all the money we had. *He* was the one doing the robbing. It was self-defence."

Nothing more was said that whole day, although Irene and Raymie exchanged looks of surprise and bewilderment at the time. Raymie would certainly want an explanation as soon as they were on their own; and Irene had none.

That tankful of gas was nearing an end when they had spotted this camp of pilgrims who were also in search of the Messiah in Montana. The campfire caught Vernon's eye first. No one in the

Lincoln had thought to bring matches, and it had turned suddenly cold. Four other cars were stopped by the fire, where people were exchanging stories about what they expected to find in Montana.

They all were showing signs of radiation sickness. Some, like Vernon, were losing hair already, and developing sores where their bodies could no longer fight infection. But they all insisted that their problems would be solved when they reached Montana and saw their Saviour.

As Irene looked at Vernon, she thought back to something Elaine had confided to her after Raymie had fallen asleep, during their second night together in the car:

"It's playing on my conscience," she had said. "You know that voice we talked about back in Illinois? The one that said 'come'? It was just a crow outside the house. I don't know if I did the right thing or not in backing Vernon up. You could describe it as sounding like 'come' as much as you could describe it as sounding like 'caw'. So when Vern said he heard Jesus say 'come', I agreed with him. It didn't take much imagination to hear it as 'come'."

Irene could not say that Elaine was entirely wrong about the "sign" from God, nor could she be entirely certain that Vernon had been wrong in reacting to the gas station owner's extortionate pricing. But it was all part of a growing disillusionment, that was starting to make her see a lot of things in a new light.

At the cloverleaf pilgrim camp, sick, weary, and dirty pilgrims were lifting themselves from makeshift beds by the fire to congregate around a late model pick-up that had driven up close to the circle. The driver had hopped up on the back to announce that he had an almost full 44-gallon drum of gasoline to sell. They weren't far from the Montana state border now, and that much gas might be enough to get someone to their destination.

Traffic was lighter going west, since most people, like the pick-up owner, were going north. The man with the gas had pumped more than he needed to reach Canada, and now he was going to sell the excess to make some easy money.

Other cars were stopped at the same cloverleaf... cars heading north on highway 85. People had come from as far south as Denver to get out of the country. People from other camps at the intersection had been alerted, and they too straggled over to join in the auction.

But few of those present had enough cash left to make a serious bid. Only three competitors were left when the price reached $1,000. They included Tom and Betty White--an elderly couple with two small grandchildren.

Irene had spoken with Tom and Betty earlier that evening. The children were orphans now. Betty had been baby-sitting them while their parents attended a function in a part of St. Paul that had sustained a direct hit.

The couple heard about the Montana Messiah from a neighbour, and they had joined the exodus. Tom had withdrawn funds for a vacation the day before the attack, so he had more cash left than others at the auction. He had, through poor planning, run out of gas just a hundred yards away from the cloverleaf. Both he and Betty were too frail to walk, and the chances of getting a ride to a gas station and back were slim in the present climate. Even if he did find a station with any gas left, there was a good chance that it would be sold out or charging more than he had by the time he could return with his car.

After re-checking his bankroll, the thin, grey-haired man called out, "Twelve hundred!" The other two bidders both indicated that they were out of the competition. The man on the pick-up motioned for Tom to bring his money over. Betty held her fists together in front of her chest and made a little jumping motion to express her happiness.

But just then, Vernon Billings walked over to the truck. He held his big left hand up for the auctioneer to look at, and he spoke quietly to him. They shook hands, and the old couple were told to put their money away. They had been outbid.

Tom and Betty walked off in tears, and sat down beside the children, who were sleeping next to Irene. "Please, take the children!" Betty begged, between sobs. "We'll give you all that we have if you'll just take the children."

Vernon was limping toward Irene, and he over-heard the conversation. He shook his head *no*, indicating with his hands that they did not have room. He signalled for Irene to leave the woman and come over to him.

"Praise the Lord!" he whispered, conspiratori-ally, when she walked up to him. "He accepted my Rolex. Irene, can you bring the car over to the pick-up, so he can fill the tank?"

"We can squeeze the children in," pleaded Irene. "Raymie and I can hold them in the back."

"And where would we put the boxes? or the water bottles?" The Billingses had loaded both the trunk and back seat up with food, clothes, and water before picking up Irene in Prospect Heights. "I can't allow that," said Vernon.

"But it's just food and clothes!" exclaimed Irene. "We're talking about two children here."

"Sister, God knows what he's doing. Just thank him for what he has done for us so far. He'll make a way for them too eventually... if it's his will. Trust God, sister. He's brought us this far."

Irene walked slowly over to the car. Trust God? she asked herself. They had trusted God that they would be taken in the rapture before all of this happened; that they would be immune to radiation; that Jesus had told them to go to Montana. And now she was supposed to trust God that two innocent children would be cared for without any sacrifice on Vernon Billings' part... or, for that matter, on her part.

Was it really God that she was being asked to trust? Or had Vernon Billings become her replacement for God? She had left her daughter, participated in an armed hold-up, and now beaten an elderly couple and two young children out of their chance for survival, just because Vernon Billings said that it was God's will.

Irene started the car and drove it up close to the pick-up. As the man with the 44-gallon drum started to siphon the gas into Vernon's car, she was overwhelmed with a desperate need for Rayford to be there and to help her with a hard decision. All her life she had known God through other people. But now she needed to make one of the most important decisions of her life, and she was being forced to do it without back-up from anyone. She tried to pray, but she lacked the certainty that Vernon Billings' confidence had always given to her in the past.

Irene waited patiently in the driver's seat while the auctioneer above her tipped his drum at an angle, and played with the hose to drain the last of it into her tank. By the time he had finished, she had made her mind up. She signalled for Pastor Billings to come over.

"Vernon," she began, calling the man by his first name for the first time. "I want you to bring that old couple over here to the car. I want to talk to them." There was a conviction in her voice that shocked Irene as much as it shocked Vernon Billings.

"It's best not to say anything..." her pastor began.

"I didn't ask your opinion. I said to *bring them here!*" she said, through clenched teeth. "Wake Raymie and bring him too." Vernon turned in shock and obeyed her. She was strangely thrilled by her own ability to make such a big decision, and to do it in the face of the man who had made so many of her decisions for her in the past. It was scary, but it was exhilarating too.

When Vernon returned, his wife was with him.

"Get in the car, Raymie," Irene said. Raymie climbed in the back, while the others gathered around the window on the driver's side. She spoke up enough so that they could all hear, but not loud enough for any other pilgrims to hear.

"There has been a change of plans. We're heading *north*," she said. "We're not going to Montana. If you want a lift to Canada, you can join us."

"No, don't say that, Sister Strait," argued Pastor Billings as he moved closer to the car. "We're almost there. We can take the children if you like..."

Just then he saw the barrel of his own pistol poking at him through the window.

"Sister Strait! What are you doing? Put that down!"

BANG! A shot rang out. It whizzed over Vernon's head. Other campers turned and looked, but assumed that the car had backfired.

"I'm serious, Vernon!" Irene said. "I've got a family back in Illinois, and I mean to find them. America has been destroyed, for whatever reason, I don't know. But I can't change things just through wishful thinking.

"Now, I'll ask just one more time: Who wants to come to Canada with me?" Tom and Betty looked timidly at each other. Their expressions suggested that their faith in the Montana myth had been teetering already. They looked back in Irene's direction and timidly raised their hands.

"Get the kids," Irene said. "It'll be crowded, but we'll do our best. What about you, Vernon? You can come with us if you like."

Vernon Billings was in deep pain--both physically and spiritually. Sweat formed on his brow as another wave of nausea swept over him. He had travelled too far down the road. His religious pride would not allow him to change directions now. Right or wrong, he was going to die for his cause. He shook his head, and then turned away to dry retch.

Irene eyed Elaine. "And you?"

"My place is with Vern," she said, as she moved closer to her fevered husband and reached out to comfort him.

"I understand," Irene said, allowing herself to soften just for a moment. "I love you... both."

The pastor's wife returned Irene's expression of love, and then Tom White got clearance from Irene before walking over to Vernon and Elaine.

He gave them the keys to his car and his roll of money while Betty loaded the kids into the car.

"My car's up there just past the overpass," Tom said, pointing to a light green Ford. "It's totally empty, but maybe you can get out of here with this." He indicated the wad of money.

Then Tom returned to Irene and joined Raymie and the older child in the back seat. Betty held the baby in the front with Irene. There were two boxes in the back too, making it quite crowded.

Irene put the car into drive, waved silently to her former pastor and his wife, and then pulled out onto the highway.

"Mom, it's too crowded back here," Raymie complained.

Irene responded slowly and deliberately as she drove, giving each word time to sink in: "I'm only going to say it once, Raymie. If you or anyone else in this car doesn't like the conditions, you just ask and I'll let you out. I'm sorry, Raymie, that I haven't taught you to be more disciplined before now. But these are dangerous times, and we all need to grow up and face reality real fast. It's time to stop complaining and to start thanking God that we are still alive, and that we have the means to get away from here. Do you understand me?"

"Yes, Mom," said Raymie. Tom and Betty also whispered acceptance of the conditions.

They drove on in silence. And as they drove, more than one of the car's occupants was praying in a way that he or she had never prayed before.

Zion Ben-Jonah Writes

The one thing that Christians need to learn most if they are to be ready for the tests that lie ahead, is how to hear and obey the voice of God. It starts with following your conscience. Because so much of the world has seared their conscience, they are rarely able to hear God's voice at all.

Obedience to God has been replaced with obedience to human authorities... parents, teachers, pastors, and police. Irene's problem was not that she obeyed Vernon Billings, or even that what Vernon Billings did was necessarily immoral. (After all, Irene herself used the gun in the end!) Her problem was just that she had failed, previously, to ask **God** what to do, or at least that she had assumed that God's will would always be revealed through her pastor. She had to actually **leave** her pastor before she could truly grow spiritually.

The religious institution tends to teach that submission to the institution will guarantee salvation, when it often happens that just the opposite is true. Salvation comes when we find a faith that is bigger than the institution.

Read Luke 17:31-37. The disciples wanted to know in advance where people should go in the last days, and Jesus gave a cryptic reply, which indicated that we each need to be like the birds, open to the subtle prompting of the Holy Spirit to tell us, minute by minute, where we should go, and when.

6. Counting the Cost

Rayford looked around the interior of the high-top Leyland Daf van. It was crowded, with four men seated in the living area, but not as crowded as he had expected. Furniture consisted of assorted cabinets and pieces of timber, all of which had come from curbside throwouts. Rayford was struck by the lack of clutter. There were places for each occupant to sleep, as well as for them to be seated. Everything else was neatly tucked away inside drawers and cupboards. Moving from one place to another inside the van was the biggest inconvenience, especially if anyone was trying to cook or do the dishes in the tiny kitchen area.

Seated next to Rayford, on a bench at right angles to the rear of the van, was the group's youngest member, 24-year-old Martin. Martin's family came from the Czech Republic. Opposite Martin and Rayford were Reinhard and Francisco. Reinhard was 32, while Francisco was 28. Fran's mother was from Argentina. Although they had not been formally trained, all three men were natural linguists. Together, they had translated *The Fall of America* into French, German, Spanish, Czech, Russian, and even Polish.

"How many of these do you get out in a week?" Rayford asked, fingering a copy of the booklet which had drawn his attention to the three men.

"Couple thousand in a good week," Martin answered. Martin was in charge of statistics. He kept the group's budget, as well as keeping records on literature stocks, distribution, rates, and accounts of where they had worked and when.

"That's 100,000 in a year," noted Rayford.

"A very *good* year," Martin reminded him.

"Whatever. The point is that even in a bad year, you should be getting new members. Why are there only three of you?"

"Two reasons," answered Francisco, who was more expressive than the other two missionaries. His hands were constantly in motion and his head would jerk in time to the movements, as though pulling the strings that moved his hands. He did it to give greater emphasis to key words, moving quickly from one thought to another.

"What we're preaching... well, people don't wanna hear... You know, they want preachers to say *soooothing* things." He dragged out the word *soothing*, while moving his hands away from one another, like a roulette croupier closing all bets. "We're talking life and death here... forsaking all... I mean giving up *everything* for God! Who wants to hear that?"

"What's the second reason people don't join you?" Rayford asked.

Reinhard answered. "Ve sink God may be *hiding us* from udder true beliefers. Dey, too, he must be hiding from *us*. One day soon ve vill come together. For now, only, he is testing us, to see if ve vill cheat, and make change to our message."

"One plants, another waters," Francisco chimed in. "The harvest will come. For now, people are reading the books. They're thinking. And they talk about it too. People tell us... every day!"

Rayford admired the idealism of this strange trio; but he could not believe that people were not joining them now that their predictions had come true about America. And he said so.

"Quickly people forget," Reinhard explained. "Dey are skeptical too. Already dey are saying dat our book vas written *after* dee attack."

"But in their hearts they know!" boasted Francisco. "They know all right! The truth is out there in those booklets, ticking away like a time bomb. One day it'll all come out. And then... ka-*POW!*" He clapped his hands together to emphasise the explosion and then shot one hand up in the air like a rocket. All three faces lit up in appreciation of what Francisco was saying.

"We're not growing in numbers; but the *truth* is getting out," said Martin quietly. "Nothing can stop the truth. And being right in *God's* eyes is more satisfying than being successful.".

"You should understand," continued Reinhard, "Ve really *belief* ven ve talk of heaven and God, and about Sheesus returning. Such faith shanges deeply our interest in udder sings. Ve are living for a new vorld... an eternal one. Our faith is not like vat ve call the *shurchy* faith."

That was an understatement! Rayford could hardly believe that a tiny band of religious fanatics living in abject poverty could have had such a deep impact on himself. Yet they were doing just that.

The truth was that he never would have given them a second thought if it had not been for the destruction of America. What a horrible price God had to pay to get his attention! Yet most of the world, even now, was more concerned about the effect on the world economy than they were about the spiritual implications of the fall of America.

Rayford stayed talking for several hours. He treated the group to a hot meal inside the Heston services, to prolong the visit. In that time, he learned that the trio parked their van most nights in service roads behind well-equipped motorway services, because they were less likely to arouse suspicion there, near 24-hour parking lots, than if they parked on city streets. Parking at the services also meant easy access to public rest rooms and showers overnight. During the day they would distribute their tracts at nearby shopping centres, just as they had done on the streets of Hounslow earlier that day.

"We don't stay at the same place two nights in a row," Martin explained. "That way, they hardly notice we're there."

The next day, Sunday, the Jesans met up with Rayford at Ruislip Country Park, for their official rest day. Rayford joined in with a group run, an informal Bible study, and a barbecue lunch, which Francisco prepared.

"Would I have to quit my job to be a true Christian?" he asked while they were eating at one of the park's few picnic tables.

"Vat you *haff* to do is to obey Sheesus," said Reinhard.

"But you just told me that he says to give up everything, and spend my time working for him!" Rayford was referring to their study of the fourteenth chapter of Luke's gospel.

"So do vat he said," Reinhard answered. "But don't yust do it because *ve* said so."

"But what about my family?"

"Vat *about* dem?" Reinhard asked quietly, raising his eyebrows as he often did to emphasise a point.

"I can't just leave them."

"So bring dem vit you."

"You know I can't do that. Chloe's trapped in Chicago, and I don't even know where Irene and Raymie are. They could be dead for all I know." Reinhard was not ignorant of this, for the Jesans had taken time to hear Rayford's story as well as to tell their own. But he wanted Rayford to see for himself how helpless he really was.

Once again Francisco's enthusiasm raced ahead of Reinhard's slower approach. "See? You're holding onto something you haven't even got!," he said. "Let go! When you do, then *God* will show you what to do. But you can't even *think* about that until you forsake them first."

Reinhard secretly signalled for Francisco to back off, leaving the group in an awkward silence for some time. They ate without speaking while Rayford engaged in a far bigger debate within his own mind. His argument was not with these relative strangers. His argument was with his Creator.

If God is real, he reasoned to himself, then God has the right to ask people to leave their families, their jobs, and their possessions to prove their faith in him. It must have been a decision like that which had freed Reinhard, Francisco, and Martin to do what they were doing now. They would never grow in numbers if others like himself did not make a similar decision. Rayford could see that talk of faith in Jesus that ignored his rules for his followers was not faith at all. But what was *he* going to do about it?

Circumstances had already taken his home and his family. All that remained was his job. Yet the job was his lifeline to his family, and his hope of getting another home one day.

"Please God," he prayed. "I can't just desert Chloe. She's counting on me."

"God knows vat is best for you," Reinhard said finally, as though reading Rayford's mind. "It is safer to take him too seriously dan to treat his vords too lightly."

Rayford was starting to sweat. He was standing at God's eternal crossroads and he knew it. He continued to pray secretly. "Help me, God. I don't want to do something stupid. There's too much at stake. What about Chloe?"

Again Reinhard spoke as though reading his mind. "Ve don't have dee control vat ve *sink* ve have," he said. "In a minute God can take avay.

And in a minute he can give back. If you vant his best, den let go! Let *God* say vat is best for you, and for da people vat you love."

Rayford Strait's analytical mind quickly weighed up the truth in what Reinhard was saying. He had told the Canadian authorities all that he knew about his family's whereabouts. Apart from that, he was powerless anyway. The real issues were the status and respect, the money, and the free-dom to travel between England and Canada that his job represented. A lot to forsake, but still nothing if it was really what God wanted. If he said no to God now, he felt certain that he would be saying no to any hope he ever had of eternal life. Rayford had been shown the truth of his spiritual condition by these men, in a way that he had never seen it before. Now he had to act on it.

Tears began to form as he yielded himself to the reality of the situation. He searched for the courage to do what his conscience told him he must do. And then his thoughts turned to the options he had for quitting his job. Should he give notice? Should he just fail to turn up? He realised then that he had made up his mind to do it... to forsake all for God. It was just a question of how... and when.

Rayford lifted his head and smiled broadly as the first tear overflowed and ran down one cheek. His companions picked up the meaning of the tear, and especially the smile that went with it. Fran-cisco, who was sitting opposite Rayford, jumped to his feet and reached out to shake his hand. The handshake quickly turned into a hug. Martin and Reinhard waited their turn to welcome him with an embrace and a few quiet tears of their own.

Rayford phoned work on Monday, to give notice. He was told that the British Army would not allow him to leave his job. It would be months before the airlines could return to normal routings, but for now every pilot and every plane was being used to maximum capacity in the evacuation.

The four men discussed the situation and agreed that Rayford's state was that of a slave... at least for the moment. He had resolved to quit his job for God, and yet circumstances had given it right back to him. He would wait until he was allowed to quit, and he would use his position in the meantime to continue to seek help for his family. While in London, he would stay with his spiritual brothers and help them get their literature out on the streets.

Over the next few weeks, along with the overwhelming concern for American suffering, Pan-Con staff also took note of a change in Rayford Strait. Rayford Strait had got religion, and had joined up with some Jesus freaks. His involvement in volunteer emergency services in Toronto was reasonable enough, but in London, he would be met at the airport by the strange young men in the Daf van and return in it a few days later, in time for his next flight out. His usual social contacts had ceased, and there was word that he was living on the streets and begging from tourists.

Zion Ben-Jonah Writes

G.K. Chesterton once said, "It is not that Christianity has been tried and found wanting. It is just that people knew it would be difficult, and so they never tried it."

The problem in the church world today is that so few people have been willing to try the simple (yet infinitely challenging) rules that Jesus laid down for his followers. We have so many religious leaders prepared to tell us what we want to hear, that we do not take time to listen to the Master himself. If the true definition of a 'Christian' is a follower of Jesus Christ, then it can hardly be said that the church is Christian, despite its generally recognised authority on religious matters.

Take time to study the fourteenth chapter of Luke, verses 25 to 35. It may be that Jesus never meant for us to take those verses literally. But it may also be that he did. So much hangs in the balance that it behooves us to pray deeply and seriously before we dismiss the implications of those verses.

When it comes to belief in a miracle of the magnitude that eternal life represents, you can be sure that we will not be able to cheat on the rules and still be able to actually experience it.

One day soon God will be asking you to lay down your **life** for him. Is it too much for you to give him your family, your job, and your wealth if he is asking for that now?

7. Refugees

Despite overwhelming tiredness, and several stops for nausea, Irene Strait made good time on her drive north from where she had left the other pilgrims in North Dakota. She drove straight through the night, arriving at the border just before noon on Saturday.

Canadian authorities were taking details from refugees as they crossed into the country, and directing them to appropriate holding camps. Tom, Betty, and their grandchildren were deemed to be in greater need of medical attention than were Irene and Raymie, so they were put on a bus and taken to Regina, where they could be given better care.

Cross-country travel was being restricted throughout Canada. Irene was totally broke, and her pleas for official help in getting to Toronto were turned down. Toronto, according to the authorities, had more than it could handle already. Irene and Raymie were, however, taken to a holding camp on the highway between Regina and Winnipeg. (They had to abandon the Lincoln at the border.) The camp was one of many being set up on farmland all over southern Canada.

Irene and Raymie would have to wait there until the situation eased in Toronto, or until they could get airlifted directly out of Saskatchewan. They were both losing hair and suffering from dehydration from so much vomiting, but they were not as sick as some others in the camp.

The refugee camp consisted of thousands of ten foot by ten foot tents, housing eight people apiece. Every four tents had one porta-potty and a small portable shower between them. Buckets inside the tents were used when the queues were too long at the toilets, or when the weather was bad. The farmland where the camp had been set up was a quagmire from recent rains and from so much pedestrian traffic.

Refugees were told to stay inside the tents to minimise further contact with fallout. Food, water, and medication for nausea, diarrhoea, and infections were brought around twice a day by untrained volunteers. Only the worst cases were referred to the understaffed medical centre on the perimeter of the camp. Two doctors supervised a small team of nurses there. Life at the camp was rough, but it was rumoured that conditions there were better than they were at many other camps.

Pan-Continental Airlines was notified by the authorities about Irene and Raymie's location and condition, and Pan-Con passed the word on to Rayford. The family had little choice but to wait on official clearance for a reunion.

For the time being, Irene and Raymie took comfort in the fact that they had safe food and water, and a tent with bunks, in which to sleep and rest, and hope. There was no way for Rayford to contact them directly, and only the most urgent outgoing calls were allowed at the camp.

Any other time, Raymie might have been whining about the conditions. They were worse than any jail in North America. But for the first two weeks he was too sick to do much more than groan as he tossed on his bunk. Only when his strength began to return did he start to complain, and even then, it was nothing compared to his old self. Irene sat pretty heavily on his complaining spirit, reminding him again and again of how lucky they were to be alive. But Raymie was genuinely trying to break his old habits too. It was like his spirit had simply been waiting for Irene to get the courage to exercise authority over it. He had been forced to do a lot of growing up in a very short period of time, and he was quickly warming to his new self-image as a disciplined and responsible adult.

The eight residents in each tent passed their time lounging on the bunks, talking, and doing various chores and calisthenics if they were strong enough. Much of the talk centred around each person's interpretation of what had transpired, and where it was all to lead, for them and for their loved ones. Virtually everyone was suffering from grief over the loss of friends and relatives, although most could only guess as to whether people outside their immediate families had survived the attack.

Normal communication links within the U.S. had totally broken down shortly after the bombings. Although there were no newspapers at the camp, some volunteers had access to news at home and they passed on what they knew when they arrived at the camp. From there, news spread quickly, by word of mouth.

The residents learned that the United Nations had taken over co-ordinating relief operations. In just a few weeks much of the surviving population of America was to be dispersed around the globe from the many holding camps in Canada and Mexico, and from airlifts within the United States... airlifts, that is, from those few places where aircraft could still come and go.

Weather patterns had been favourable, blowing most of the fallout out over the Atlantic. An Arctic cold front three days after the attack pushed air southward and kept most of the fallout away from Canada. Even so, radiation levels in southern Canada were still far above normal. Canadians had been cautioned to stay inside as much as possible. The rest of the world, apart from islands in the Caribbean, and some parts of Mexico, was assured that the radiation threat to them was minimal.

Russia's attitude toward the war was to act as though it had never happened. As soon as her bombers had completed their missions, blowing up military installations and other key centres of transportation, power, and communication, they had returned to their bases. From that point on, Russia had offered as much aid to the survivors as anyone else.

The U.S. and England had both been officially expelled from the U.N. just days after the attack. America was dropped ostensibly because it ceased to exist; but almost no explanation was given for dumping England. Despite protests from the British, there was hardly any objection from other member nations. The expulsion had not been accompanied by any sanctions against Britain, and the British were so preoccupied with assisting Americans that they did not have much time or interest in taking on the U.N. in the face of such overwhelming opposition from the rest of the world.

Loss of American trade was a threat to the economy of many smaller nations, but the U.N. started to work immediately on programs to re-claim land owned by American interests, and to re-cultivate it so that it could carry products which would better meet the needs of the local populations. The same thing was being done with American industrial interests. Secretary General Dangchao promised to actually *increase* wealth for the Third World. The World Bank was surprisingly co-operative with his proposals.

An economic summit was being planned to consider various proposals for stabilising the world economy. Talk of a single currency was a key issue on the agenda.

One sphere of activity at the U.N. which was not getting as much media coverage as the eco-nomic and political changes, was a plan for a world religious summit. The masses of the world longed for reassurance that the disaster in the U.S. was not going to be repeated; and religious leaders had been shocked into overlooking many of the differences that had previously divided them. They too wanted to play their part in promoting worldwide co-operation... co-operation with one another, as well as co-operation with the quickly evolving world government. In times of crisis people invariably turn to religion for comfort and direction; so it was important for the government and the churches, synagogues, mosques, and temples to provide a unified (and unifying) image of hope and peace.

No word had been received at all from President Fitzhugh, who, with his family and aids, had been trapped under the White House when it was bombed. Hopes were fading that they had survived the blast, even though a series of tunnels existed under the building, and it was believed that he had been rushed there several minutes before the bomb hit. Under normal circumstances there would have been a system for appointing a replacement for the President, but the Vice-President and several other potential successors were dead or missing, along with a sizeable proportion of the Senators and Congressmen who would have to oversee such a decision. Most of those who *were* alive, were little more than refugees themselves. Truly America had ceased to exist as an independent nation.

The U.S.'s unwavering support for Israel had been that country's mainstay for many years. The tiny Jewish state, surrounded as it was by Arab nations, was understandably nervous about the shift in power. But Dangchao surprised the world and gained respect for his sense of fair play by putting peace talks between Israel and the Arab states high on his priorities. It was rumoured that Jewish influences in the World Bank were what really won Dangchao over. He was getting many billions of dollars in support from the World Bank for his Third World plans. In exchange the U.N. was taking a decidedly pro-Israeli position in the peace talks.

But, sadly, for the millions of Americans still struggling to escape the death and destruction that had ravaged that country, developments in world politics were incidental to their daily quest for survival. Tens of thousands were continuing to die each day from injuries received in the initial blasts, some of them dying without any medical aid at all. Many had been left where they fell, to suffer for days before finally succumbing. A few had been carried away, only to die on the road, in refugee camps, or in hospitals. Burials were rare. Cremations were faster. But in most cases bodies were left to rot, and disease was left to spread, as survivors had fled the scene.

For people like Chloe, still waiting for help to reach her, the threat of catching cholera or typhoid was now the biggest worry.

Zion Ben-Jonah Writes

Two symbols are used for America in Bible prophecy: a prostitute named Babylon, and the Eagle's wings on the back of a Lion (the Lion being the symbol for England). (See notes at the end of chapter 2.)

In Daniel 7:4, the Eagle's wings are plucked, and the Lion (i.e. England) ceases to be a "beast" (or world empire) as a result. In Revelation 17:16-18, and all of Revelation 18, we read of the fall of Babylon, and how it affects the kings, merchants, and shipping companies of the world.

Remember, however, that the term "Babylon" not only refers to America. It is a symbol for all of the empires of man. And so the title will eventually pass on to the new centre of world economics, under the new world order.

The rise of a single world religion may or may not be assisted by the United Nations. Moves toward ecumenicalism have been underway for some time now; but disasters always have a way of bringing the masses back to thoughts of religion, and of bringing religious leaders together with one another.

America's obsession with Israel is usually explained to the masses (thanks to the churches) on the basis that they are God's "chosen people" (despite the fact that they rejected God's Son... their Messiah!). However, interest in Israel at government levels has always had more to do with their control of world banking.

8. Reunion

Chloe had worked hard at making her stay in Prospect Heights both safe and stable. She arranged to turn the satphone on for just a few hours each week--the times when her father was most confident of being able to contact her. She increased her water supply by retrieving water from the toilets upstairs. When that was depleted, she made her first and only venture outside, to get water and food from two neighbouring houses which had been deserted shortly after the attack. She moved out of the basement in the second week and back into the rooms on the ground floor. But she continued to use the basement as her latrine. Because there were no deaths in her immediate vicinity, she was safe from disease as long as she did not travel too far afield. Overall, she spent her last week at Prospect Heights in relative comfort.

Just three weeks after the attack a rescue bus pulled up in front of the house and offered Chloe a lift to a ferry that would take her and hundreds of other survivors up Lake Michigan to Port Elgin, on the east side of Lake Huron. From there, they were taken by bus to holding camps near Toronto.

Chloe was only in the camp for two days before she was taken to the airport. She had not heard from her father for five days, but she was not surprised when she was issued with a ticket on a Pan-Con flight to London. She was also not surprised when she found her father waiting for her after she had passed through airport security

... but she certainly was excited. They embraced and rejoiced, backing off so that they could look at each other before embracing again. The stress of the past weeks erupted in profuse tears for Chloe. But she sensed that her father was still holding something back.

"Any word on Mom and Raymie?" she asked

"They're fine," Rayford said. "They're still in Regina, but it shouldn't be long. I've signed papers for them to come to England when they're released."

But Rayford's thoughts were on something else.

"Chloe, can you sit in the cockpit with me today?" he asked.

"Are you kidding? No one could keep me from it!" she giggled.

Rayford added, "I've made some important decisions about serving God. We need to talk about it."

Chloe had been doing a lot of praying herself, so she could appreciate what she thought was her father's decision to attend church. "I understand," she said with a smile as they walked to the plane. She reached out and squeezed his hand, grateful to have him near her once again.

"There's more to it than you probably realise," he said. "We'll talk about it after takeoff."

Inside the plane, Rayford was totally occupied with routine safety checks, communication (both with the control tower and with the passengers), and with flying the aircraft. But when they were at cruising altitude and the seat belt sign had been turned off, Rayford handed control over to his copilot and moved to the navigator's seat, where he and Chloe could talk more privately.

"There's so much I need to say," he began. "First off, you should know that I personaly don't have a house or even a room in London."

"We'll manage. I'll get a job," Chloe promised.

Rayford searched for words to tell her the depth of his new commitment.

"We don't need jobs," he said. "In fact, I'll be quitting this job soon... to work for God."

Chloe's eyes opened wide. Something strange was going on.

"Quit your job?" she asked in amazement. "How would we survive? You're not even trained to be a *preacher*." She said the word "preacher" with a bit of a sneer.

"But I already *am* a preacher," Rayford replied.

"Where? What church?"

"No church. I just talk to people about God... on the street."

"What? You mean you're a *street* preacher?" Things were looking stranger still.

"No, I just offer literature to people, and sometimes they stop and talk."

How embarrassing, thought Chloe. Her father --a distinguished airline pilot--spruiking on street corners. She continued to picture him shouting to an indifferent crowd, with a Bible in his hand. But she tried to hide her feelings.

"You don't need to quit your job," she said. "With what you earn, you could pay someone else to do it, and we could still put our family back together again."

"Chloe, honey," began Rayford. "Can you give me a few minutes to explain? It's very important to me for you to know exactly what's happening."

Chloe was genuinely keen to get the bigger picture. "Sure," she said sympathetically. "Go ahead." She settled back in her seat to listen.

Rayford began at his airport encounter with Reinhard, hours after the attack. He told of how he had always felt that religion as taught in the churches was shallow and escapist. But he admitted that he too had been shallow and evasive when it came to the things of God.

"These guys in the van got me reading what Jesus actually taught," he said.

Chloe had never responded to religion as taught by her mother, so Rayford knew he could not reason with her as he would with Irene. He needed to start with something more basic.

"You can't tell me that what you've been through these past three weeks hasn't made you think about God," he said with a knowing smile.

Chloe nodded. She had often prayed for help, especially during those first few days in the basement. But prayer for her was something that you only did when all else failed. It wasn't fair to burden God with things you could work out for yourself.

"Well, I've come to see that our whole existence is part of a plan... sort of a test... where God watches to see if we'll serve him or if we're going to insist on doing our own thing."

Then Rayford appeared to shift tack for a moment. "All the prayers in the world won't keep us from dying one day. Yet most of our prayers seem to be asking for just that... prayers that we will not suffer, not die, or just not be too inconvenienced." Rayford felt that he was not making himself clear.

"What I'm trying to say is that, if we're going to pray at all, we need to be asking for something other than selfish things."

There was an interruption as a stewardess came in with coffee. Chloe accepted a cup and added sugar, but she was distracted mentally, trying to make sense of what had happened to her father. She could not get the picture out of her mind of Rayford standing on a street corner and shouting to the public. How could he seriously think that he should serve God in that way? Nobody listens to street preachers! If her dad really wanted to preach, he should do it through a church. He was too smart to be preaching on the streets. Had he snapped, under the pressure of the war?

Chloe was pulled out of her reverie when Rayford resumed talking.

"Honey, I'd give anything to get you to see what I've seen. But with or without your support, I really have to go through with what I believe God wants me to do." No response. So Rayford went on.

"We weren't put here to work for money. We were put here to work for God. When you accept that, it's easy to see how virtually all of the world's problems have come from greed. I've been living on almost nothing for the past two weeks, and I feel more alive than I ever have before."

"That's easy to say when Pan-Con pays your hotel bill," Chloe argued. "And who gets your paycheck? This Reinhard guy? Sounds like a scam to me."

"Reinhard holds the money, but he's not spending it selfishly. And I haven't been staying at the hotel in London. Pan-Con isn't even *feeding* me when I'm in England."

Rayford made several attempts to get Chloe to see the *spiritual* importance of what he had discovered, but she could not be pulled away from the material issues, and he didn't like being put on the defensive about his faith.

"We've got a room for you, Mom, and Raymie with a friend in Guildford," he said. "You'll have to share it with Raymie and Mom when they get there. It's almost impossible to get cheap accommodation with all the new arrivals."

"And where are *you* going to stay?" Chloe asked. Her attitude was changing from shock to anger, as the extent of her father's commitment dawned on her.

"I'll be staying in the van with the other guys," he said. "That's part of what I've been trying to tell you."

"What kind of a God is that?" Chloe half shouted. Her face was screwed up in anger. "He wouldn't tell you to leave your family... not *now*, when we need you so much." And tears began to form in her eyes.

Rayford's heart was breaking. He had always been close to Chloe, and he had hoped that she would be more understanding about something that meant so much to him. He decided to let her think things over, while he tended to official duties in the pilot's seat for an hour or so.

When he returned to the seat beside Chloe, she was much calmer. She had brushed away her tears.

"Okay," she began when he was seated. "Let's say that God really does want you to do this. What do you think he would want me and Mom and Raymie to do?"

That was the Chloe that Rayford had remembered. Her head was ruling her heart now. She must have seen where her negative reactions were leading and decided to take a more constructive approach. Chloe's respect and admiration for her father was helping her to treat his extreme lifestyle change as a genuine decision on his part, even if she could not agree with it herself.

"Honey, I'd love to think that God wants you to *join* me. But you really have to find that out for yourself."

Chloe worked her way slowly through a list of questions she had about how Rayford had reached his bizarre conclusions. But this time she tried to listen, and she tried to feel what her father was feeling. Everything was making more sense when she did it that way.

Rayford explained how the loss of so many lives (including many personal friends and relatives) in America, and the possibility that he could lose his wife and children as well, had made him seriously question all of his values.

"All the money in the world won't guarantee that I can hang onto you, Mom, and Raymie," he said. "And it would be even more useless when I stand before God. I know that what I'm doing sounds crazy to most people; but what's *really* crazy is ignoring eternal things, like most of us do most of the time.

"God doesn't need money," he continued. "He made the world without it, and he can keep things *going* without it too. See, Jesus talked of something called God's world, or God's kingdom, where people work for love instead of working for money. It's like a return to the Garden of Eden... God's original plan for the human race."

Rayford looked deep into his daughter's eyes. His heart was pounding in excitement. She was really listening!

"I know you can see at least *some* of what I'm saying," he said quietly and with deep feeling. "But if you actually started living it like I've been doing for the past couple of weeks, it would all make ten times more sense."

Chloe was thinking ahead. "Well, suppose we *were* to come with you. Where would we stay? How much room *is* there in that van of yours?"

Rayford laughed as he answered the question, more from relief at hearing Chloe mention the possibility of coming with him, than at her question. He fought to keep his secret hopes from getting ahead of her. "No way! We'd never fit in the van," he laughed. "It's pretty crowded as it is. But God would make a way for us somewhere."

"I'm not saying that you've convinced me," Chloe cautioned. "But I don't want to lose you either." The truth was that she still thought he may have been sucked in by a cult; but she didn't want to go back to arguing. If she could check it out for herself, that would be better.

"For now you can move in with Neville and Mary in Guildford," Rayford said. "They're an elderly couple who have supported the team for a few years now. They have an extra bedroom that they let us use when we're in the area. We'll have plenty of opportunity to visit you and for you to visit with us."

When the plane landed in London, the guys met Rayford as usual. Fran grabbed Chloe's bag and they all stood around talking for some time while Reinhard left to get the van. "Parking is too expensive at the airport, but we know a place a few blocks away where we can park for free," Rayford explained. "Reinhard won't be long."

Chloe was surprised at her father's miserly approach to such a minor thing as an airport parking fee. But over the next few weeks she would see many more examples of how the men had learned to survive on almost no cash in a world where everyone else spent freely. They called it being "poor in spirit".

The van was smaller than she had expected, but the other members of her father's 'team' were nicer and more normal than she had expected. The room at Neville's and Mary's was adequate-- especially when she compared it to her stay in the basement at Prospect Heights. Food was plentiful, as were fresh water and clean clothes. If nothing else, she had learned to appreciate little things more over the past three weeks.

During the next four days, before Rayford was to fly out once again, the Jesans made as much time available for Chloe as she wanted to take. She was impressed with their genuine concern for her welfare. She learned that Reinhard had been saving up Rayford's pay from Pan-Con, and he already had enough to rent a small apartment for the Straits after Irene and Raymie arrived. The men wanted to consult Chloe's mother and brother before making a decision on where she was going to live.

It was three more weeks before mother and son were released from their holding camp. In that time, Chloe had become quite comfortable with her father's new companions.

"Funny, isn't it?" she said to Rayford one evening as she relaxed with him at the services near Guildford after he had completed his stint of distributing tracts for the day. "We live our whole life in fear of poverty; but poverty's not so bad at all, is it?"

"Not if you call this poverty," said her father from across the table. He grabbed another handful of peanuts from a bowl on the table. "All the money in the world doesn't do much more than feed, clothe and house us. And we have that already."

* * *

Irene and Raymie had been taken by bus to Toronto, but they missed Pan-Con's morning flight to London by one hour. So they were put on a British Airways flight later that night. When they arrived, early the following morning, the other men stayed out of sight, while Rayford and Chloe waited to meet Irene and Raymie. Mother and son had both lost weight, and their hair was just starting to grow back. Irene kept her head covered with a scarf, but Raymie seemed proud of his new skinhead look.

They were exhausted from the flight, so Rayford did not try to discuss his plans on the way to Neville's. Shortly after they arrived in Guildford, both Irene and Raymie fell asleep.

It was almost noon when Irene woke up and stumbled into Neville's big living room. Rayford, Chloe, Neville, Mary, and the other Jesans were all gathered there. Rayford introduced Irene, and she caught them up with what she and Raymie had been through since they left Prospect Heights.

Rayford had been planning to talk to Irene privately about his plans, but the subject came up in the course of introducing the other Jesans.

Rayford had Chloe's qualified endorsement, but he also had the advantage of Irene's prior commitment to Christian faith. More than anything, what helped him was Irene's dramatic change on the clover leaf in North Dakota. It had broken the spell that Vernon Billings and traditional Christianity had over her. And now her husband was offering her a new purpose for living. More than that, he was offering her something that was truly Christian. She listened intently and tried not to panic at what Rayford was suggesting.

Over the next few weeks, Irene, Chloe, and Raymie progressed from being co-operative with Rayford, to deeply respecting him, to adopting his faith for their own. There was no single moment when it happened, but the more they studied, discussed, or even thought about the teachings of Jesus, the more their faith grew. They unanimously chose to join the Jesans.

A month after Irene returned, Rayford was released from his obligation to stay with Pan-Con. A group decision was made to use the money they had been saving for an apartment to buy another van for Chloe and Raymie instead. They would use it in their new job as Jesan tract distributors.

Neville and Mary had become quite fond of Rayford and Irene, and they insisted that the couple use the second bedroom at their apartment on a permanent basis.

From that point on, life for the Jesans took a dramatic turn.

Zion Ben-Jonah Writes

Whatever else religious formulas for conversion may include, they all seem to leave out the essential ingredient, which is the teachings of Jesus. In this chapter, we have people listening to and responding to the teachings of Jesus, and the result in each case is a dramatic change in lifestyle.

Jesus said that the religious builders would leave out the Cornerstone of his teachings, and that the result would be like that of a foolish person building a house on sand. Whatever it is that they are trying to build, he said, would eventually collapse. But he said that any who would listen to his teachings and at least <u>seek</u> to obey him, would be like a wise person building on a rock... the storms and floods of this life and of the next would not be able to shake them.

This is the message of salvation that <u>Jesus</u> taught, and it is the one that we should be teaching today.

Jesus said that, if we are faithful to share his teachings with others, then anyone who accepts us and what we are saying will, in effect, be accepting him and what he taught. (Matthew 10:40) In this chapter, Chloe, Irene, and Raymie had to start by accepting what Rayford (and then Reinhard and the others) said in defence of Jesus and his teachings. As they did, they were 'born again" by the "Word of God", which is actually the Bible's name for Jesus. (See Revelation 19:13-16.)

BOOK TWO

9. The Countdown Begins

"Another one!" Rayford exclaimed to himself as he sat at his desk late one night in January.

It had been eighteen months since the Straits had joined the Jesans. Rayford's keen interest in Bible prophecy, and his natural aptitude for teaching had catapulted him to a leadership role in the tiny community. He wondered how he could have ever been happy as an airline pilot. Life had been so exciting since he had made the dramatic decision to let go and give everything to God.

Rayford's role in the community had triggered a commitment from Neville too, who was thrilled to be able to work full-time with Rayford on something he was good at... computers. Neville was like a young man again, and Mary, who hardly ever said a word, was happy to see the change in her husband.

The two men had been working together for more than a year, with Rayford producing articles on a wide range of topics (but especially on how each topic related to what was happening in world events at that time), and with Neville setting up a web page where people could go to access all of the material that Rayford was producing. Some days Rayford would produce four or five articles in a single day. Much of the inspiration for them came from his involvement with the rest of the Jesans, and from thoughts which they shared from their stints out on the streets.

Neville installed a guest book, a hit counter, an internal search engine, and a tracker on their home page. He also developed an automatic study course, which would test people on a list of questions from one article before directing them to the next one. Neville made sure that the page was well represented on search engines all over the world, and he collected thousands of email addresses for a worldwide newsletter which Chloe and Reinhard produced once a month. The newsletter aimed at stimulating enough curiosity to get people to visit their web site.

"Look at this," Rayford said when he had finished reading the papers he had in his hands. He spun the chair around and shoved them toward Irene. "Six letters in today's snail mail, and they all sound like genuine seekers. Wouldn't it be great to get a new member out of this?"

Rayford had come to see the truth in the group's theory that God was deliberately blocking people from joining them. They had not had a new member since he had joined, and he had tried everything he could think of to locate the problem. About once a week they would get a promising letter from someone who had read one of their tracts or visited their website. But they rarely heard from these people again. Getting six serious enquiries in one day was unprecedented.

Irene skim read the letters and then spoke. "Sounds great, doesn't it? What do you plan to do with them?"

"Neville and Mary will be away next week. I may try to get all six of them here on Monday. Then I won't have to answer the same questions over and over."

"Do you think it's wise to bring them here?" asked Irene. The group had a policy of not giving out Neville's address until they first checked people out.

"I have a feeling about this," Rayford said. "I think there's a connection between this and the talks in Jerusalem."

Rayford was talking about a U.N. plan to construct a Temple in Jerusalem for the Jews. The world was gradually recovering from the destruction of America, and now there was time for people to consider other matters. Talks had been going on in Israel for the past two or three weeks. Secretary General Dangchao himself had been there for the past three days, and even the Pope was participating.

The Arabs had been adamant that there would be all-out war if anyone dared to touch the Dome of the Rock, their most sacred mosque. It had been built centuries earlier, almost on the original site of Solomon's Temple, where Jews had for centuries offered sacrifices to God. However, Dangchao had come up with a compromise package. It involved construction of a Jewish Temple on one side of the Dome of the Rock and a matching Christian temple on the other side. The sacred Muslim mosque itself would not be touched. The newly elected Pope Pius XIII had hinted that he was prepared to move from the Vatican to take up residence in Jerusalem, not far from the new Temple, as a symbol of Vatican commitment to this historic step toward religious unity.

Muslims were not thrilled about the offer, but there was something in Dangchao's manner that suggested he would not take No for an answer.

If people had thought that the Americans were biased in favour of the Jews, the Americans looked positively wishy washy by comparison to Dangchao. U.N. troops had been increased in the holy city, and Muslims took it as a warning of what Dangchao might do if they turned down his Temple "offer".

"Talks in Jerusalem? I can't remember a time when there hasn't been some sort of talk making news in the Middle East," Irene commented.

"I know what you mean," Rayford answered. "Before I became a Jesan, I used to wonder why there was so much interest in those talks. Must've been because people in the know were looking for hints of the 'agreement' even back then. Now, after all these years, we could be about to witness the real thing. If Dangchao pulls it off, it could confirm what I've been thinking about him.

What Rayford had been thinking was that Xu Dangchao was the prophesied Antichrist. The one problem had been his name. According to Bible prophecy (Revelation 13:17-18), the numeric value of the letters in the name of the world's final ruler should add up to 666. Whatever system Rayford used (Greek, Hebrew, Latin, or even Dangchao's native Chinese), the value of the letters in his name fell short.

The only <u>Roman</u> numerals, for example, were X, D, and C, which equalled 610. The letters I, V, and L were needed, to make up the missing 56.* In Greek and Hebrew tallies, the figures were even farther out. Rayford did not know what to make of it. Yet there were other things that pointed to Xu Dangchao being the prophesied Antichrist.

Dangchao's success in taking control of the world through the U.N. was a hint of his special role, although here too, Rayford had to admit that the nations of the world were not officially controlled by the United Nations yet. They still continued to operate independently of one another.

Nevertheless, Dangchao had built up U.N. military might to the point where U.N. troops were deployed in great numbers throughout the world. Because of their presence, the world had experienced total peace, if not total unity, during the year and a half since the collapse of America.

If Secretary General Dangchao were to succeed in getting a Temple for the Jews, then not only would

_____

*The letters I, V, X, L, C, and D (Roman numerals for 1, 5, 10, 50, 100, and 500) must all appear once (and only once), and the letter M (1,000) must not appear at all for a name to add up to 666 in Roman numerals.

Note: The names used in this book are totally fictitious. It is possible that the real Antichrist will have a name that adds up to 666 based on the numerical value of Latin, Greek <u>and</u> Hebrew letters.

Rayford be convinced that he was the Antichrist, but he would also be able to compute the exact number of days until Jesus would return.

Rayford was up late that night studying the six letters that he had received, and thinking about the proposed meeting on Monday. He refused meals on Saturday and Sunday, spending most of his time alone in his room or outside walking. He said only enough to Irene to let her know that nothing was wrong, either between the two of them or between Rayford and God. Instead, his intense meditation sprang from a sober anticipation about what God might be about to do.

When he phoned the enquirers on Saturday, Rayford found them all to be co-operative and hopeful. John Doorman and Sister Mary Teresa had jobs that allowed them to set their own hours. Matthew Baker and Sheila Armitage had no job. And the other two said they would take the day off on Monday, to be in on the meeting.

John Doorman was a 42-year-old Jehovah's Witness who found the Jesan interpretation of prophecy appealing. The Jesans taught that all governments were inherently evil, and that God was looking for a loyalty to himself that would transcend political issues. Doorman was also a pacifist. He had worked for a while as a missionary in his native Africa, where he had been jailed for a number of years for his beliefs. He had never been married, and he worked part-time as a handyman in order to make more time available for his church work.

Sister Mary Teresa was a 56-year-old Catholic nun with the Little Sisters of Jesus. She lived and worked with migrants in one of the poorest suburbs of London. She was attracted to the simple community lifestyle of the Jesans, and their idea of building a community composed of married couples and families, as well as celibate singles.

Matthew Baker was a 40-year-old Baptist who kept himself busy visiting hospitals and prisons, and passing out tracts on the streets. He was zealous about many moral issues and showed special appreciation for the Jesan stand on marriage and divorce. His wife had left him in the second year of their marriage, because she objected to his religious beliefs.

Sheila Armitage was a 70-year-old Quaker lesbian who was drawn to the group's tolerance of other religions, and their teaching that sincerity means more to God than theology.

Mike Anastopoulos was a 36-year-old student from Turkey, who was doing a doctorate in archaeology. He had no religious affiliation, but referred to himself as a humanist. Mike expressed interest in what the Jesan community was saying about economics in general, and about survival outside of the economic and political system in particular.

Finally, there was Luis Rafael, a 29-year-old Pentecostal migrant from Brazil. He had, two years earlier, joined The Family, a radical Pentecostal community with controversial teachings about sex. Luis liked The Family's teachings on Bible prophecy and living by faith, but he had become disillusioned with some of their other teachings. He liked the Jesans' literal approach to the teachings of Jesus, and their tendency to use them as the standard by which to measure all other teachings.

Rayford had read through all of their letters several times on Friday night, and he had discussed some of the issues that interested each of them in his phone calls on Saturday. All six sounded like they were genuinely hungering after more truth, although there were the usual disturbing signs of prejudice in each of them as well. He prayed that God would give him the wisdom to deal with these prejudices as they came up on Monday.

*   *   *

Luis Rafael was the first to arrive on Monday morning. But Rayford had barely introduced him to Irene before the doorbell rang again... and again. By ten o'clock, all six seekers were nervously seated in Neville's living room.

"Let's see... Where shall we begin?" Rayford mumbled, half to himself. "How about if *you* start, by asking any questions you might have, and we'll do our best to answer them." He glanced over at Irene, as though looking for support.

Mike Anastopoulos, the agnostic archaeologist, had learned enough during the introductions to know that all of the others had religious affiliations. He spoke first. "Do we have to believe in God to be part of this group?"

"It depends on what you mean by believing in

God," Rayford replied. He saw an immediate reaction from both Matthew and Luis, the two evangelical Christians in the room. They both shifted forward in their seats to better hear what Rayford was about to say.

"Theology doesn't save us," he said. "What saves us is faith in the highest revelation of God that we know. Call it love or truth if you like, but we call it God."

Mike seemed happy with that answer, but Matthew and Luis exchanged glances before Luis raised his hand to speak.

"I disagree," he said. "If someone's really sincere, then they would *have to* believe in God."

John Doorman had reached into a briefcase that stood beside his chair, pulling out a small magazine, which he offered to Mike. "Jehovah God wants everyone to know him by name," he said. "There's an article in here that will help you."

"Is that a *Watchtower* magazine?" asked Matthew. "Are you a Jehovah's Witness?"

"Uh-oh," thought Rayford. This had been what he most wanted to avoid. Jehovah's Witnesses were despised by most mainline Christian denominations. All this enthusiasm in one room could accomplish powerful things for God, but only if it could be made to work in harmony. Already it was taking a turn that Rayford had seen religious zeal take many times before. He had believed that God was going to work a miracle today, but things were not looking that way at the moment.

"Yes, I am a witness for Jehovah," replied John Doorman, sticking his chin out with pride.

"And what about you?" Matthew Baker said, addressing Sister Mary Teresa. "I take it, from the way you're dressed, that you're a Catholic. Do you pray to Mary?"

"Well, I..." Sister Mary was lost for words.

"You see what's happening here?" Mike interjected, standing and pointing at Matthew. "This is why I never had any time for religion. Nothing but arguments and nit-picking. Here, take your magazine. I'm not interested." He handed the *Watchtower* back to John Doorman.

"Maybe we should all just..." Sheila began, hoping to calm people down; but she was interrupted, as Mike continued:

"I didn't come to hear what the rest of you have to say. I came to hear what the *Jesans* have to say!"

"It doesn't matter what the Jesans believe," shouted Luis, who had also jumped to his feet. "What matters is what the *Bible* says."

"And what if I don't happen to *believe* the Bible?" asked Mike, *his* chin out this time.

"Then maybe you don't belong here!" Matthew replied, also jumping to his feet, and taking a step in Mike's direction as he spoke.

Sheila quickly jumped between the two men, extending her arms in both directions, as though separating boxing opponents. "Why don't we just sit down and..."

But Luis spoke over top of her. "The Bible says,

in Acts 4:12, "Neither is there salvation in any other; for there is none other name under heaven..."

"ENOUGH!"

There was disagreement about exactly what happened at that instant. Some of those present could not even agree as to whether Rayford said anything at all.

"It was more like an explosion," Luis said later, "except that it came out of his mouth."

Whatever it was, it sent people literally flying across the room and into one another. Sister Mary, the only one still seated at the time, had tipped over backwards in her chair. Only Irene, who was standing behind Rayford when it happened, escaped the blast. Some of the others had bruises from it. A flash of light had accompanied the explosion. It had filled the room and momentarily blinded everyone present.

Rayford himself was as shocked as anyone. But then he began to speak -- with an authority that he had never experienced before. It scared him, but it would have scared him even more *not* to have spoken, for he knew that what was coming out of his mouth at that moment was not his own words. They were the very words of God.

And when he spoke, the entire room was silent. People *listened* as they had never listened to anyone before.

"You are not here today because your doctrines are right. *God* has brought you here; and he has only done it because you are *sincere*. For two thousand years he has tolerated, and even engineered some of the divisions that have existed between you and other believers. Many of you have preached your half-baked doctrines, believing that you had the whole picture, when you only had a part of it. You have promoted personalities and organisations in your ignorance. And you imagined that people following other doctrines and leaders and organisations were somehow inferior to yourselves.

"God left you ignorant, in most cases, to test your loyalty to *him*. He wanted to know if you would stay true to what you believed, even if it alienated you from your friends and family. And you are here today because you have each passed that test."

Then Rayford raised his voice again. "But NOW... now, it's time to grow up!" Some of those present scooted back from where they were sitting on the floor. They were cringing in expectation of another explosion.

But it never came. Rayford's voice softened instead.

"Please believe me. Your single claim to righteousness is the grace of God. He has chosen you entirely because of your sincerity -- not because of your theology... or your lack of it." He looked at Mike as he said the last few words.

Rayford picked up a stack of three-ring binders and proceeded to pass them out to the six people cowering in front of him. Over the past year, he had worked long hours to produce the material in those notebooks.

"There are articles in here on a wide range of topics," he said. "You are going to find some of them shocking. They will challenge some of your most sacred dogmas.

"Brothers and sisters," he said with a pause and a hint of a smile, "it's time to move into a deeper understanding of truth than any of you have ever known before. It's time to prove your sincerity by *listening* to one another, and by setting aside your prejudices when you do."

Rayford then tried to give the assembly a bigger picture of the significance of the moment.

"A treaty is being signed in Jerusalem today," he said. "Before sundown tonight, construction will begin on a new Temple in Jerusalem. But a far greater agreement has been made in heaven. God is going to build *his* Temple, and, believe it or not, he's going to use you people here to do it. We have entered the final seven years of church history. The Great Tribulation is just three and a half years away, and it is our job to prepare the world for that time."

Rayford paused again, to let the gravity of the situation sink in. Then he continued.

"The death of Jesus marked the end of organised religion. God has, for two thousand years, been dealing with people personally and individually, trying to build character and faith that goes beyond organisational affiliation.

"But now he's going to put all of the best qualities and bits of truth together to build *his* church, and not your own."

Mike, the humanist, was pleased to hear Rayford talking about things like individualism and character; but he was battling with the idea that this was all coming from a real God -- and a Christian one at that. Words like "church" and "Jesus" were hard for him to swallow. Mike was a bit of an anarchist too, and so talk of a new organisation also unnerved him.

In one way or another, each person in the room was facing a similar battle. They had been thrown together with people whom they had, for one reason or another, regarded as the enemy. But the presence of God there told them that Rayford was not just another guru trying to start another denomination.

Rayford went on: "Right now, in another part of the world, there is another meeting going on like this one. There are six other people like yourselves. One is a Hindu, one a Muslim, and one a Jew." What Rayford was saying came not from his own human understanding, but rather, he was speaking, as he had been from the initial shout, as the mouth of God.

"If you think *you* have differences to overcome, imagine how it must be for them. But God wants you people here and the six people he has brought together elsewhere to actually *lead* his endtime church through what lies ahead. You will become the 'judges' of this great movement. But you'll need to overcome your differences in order to do that.

"God's original plan for his people was for them to have twelve tribes, with tribal judges, to sort out problems as they arose. Not kings. Not dictators. But just tribal judges... people like Samuel, and

Gideon, and Deborah." He glanced at Sheila and Sister Mary Teresa as he mentioned Deborah.

"Your job will be to help believers in your area of the world to know what is right and what is wrong. You won't be able to *do* that until you can overcome your differences, and until you can recognise the limitations of your own understanding."

Rayford could feel the anointing fading, and he spoke more as an equal with those present now.

"Brothers and sisters, I don't have all the answers. What I have prepared in these notebooks can act as a guide. But the bottom line is that you are going to have to learn how to hear God telling you things that you don't want to hear. You are going to have to learn to look past your own prejudices. We have a lot to learn in a very short period of time.

"We're going to try talking once again, but I want each of you to work harder at listening this time, and to pray long and hard before you speak. You each have something to contribute, but it may not be as much as you *think* you have."

The entire atmosphere in the room had been transformed. Everyone was subdued... humbled by the truth in what Rayford had said, and by the overwhelming presence of God in that room. Little by little they broached some of the issues that separated them; but they did so timidly this time. When tensions arose, they would retreat into more prayer for more grace in their dealings with each other.

And so the Western half of the Twelve Tribes , as the movement came to be called, was born.

Zion Ben-Jonah Writes

The Hebrew prophet, Daniel, gave a remarkable prediction about "God's people" 453 years before Jesus was born. (Daniel 9:24-26) He said that there were 490 years left for God's people, but that their Messiah would be "cut off" seven years before those 490 years were completed, in 30 A.D. (See "Armageddon for Beginners", chapter 6, "The Seventy Weeks", for a detailed discussion of that passage.)

The crucifixion of Jesus marked the end of organised religion as such. God has, for nearly two thousand years dealt with people individually and personally. All attempts at promoting "one true church" have ended in travesties of the "kingdom of heaven", which Jesus said was invisible. (Luke 17:20)

However, Daniel said that God's people would become a visible organisation once again as a result of an "agreement" made seven years before the "consummation" of all things. (Daniel 9:27) The prophecy is written in such a way as to indicate two parallel agreements. One is made between Christ and his Church, and the other is made between Antichrist and his Church.

The agreement will result in sacrifices once again being made in the (presently non-existent) Temple in Jerusalem... at least for the first three and a half years of that agreement. And it will also result in the coming together of twelve "tribes" of Christian believers.

10. Twelve Tribes

Discussion continued for the rest of the day. Each of the six people present in Neville's living room had a lifetime of experience to un-learn. By the end of the day they were starting to feel the enormity and the urgency of this little experiment. Their religious affiliations, jobs, and families faded in importance, as they grew in their conviction about what God was doing.

Irene provided food throughout the day, as well as making cushions and blankets available when the group spontaneously decided to stay on at Neville's until they were clear about what God's next step was to be for them. Some of them talked far into the night, pumped up on the excitement of so much new revelation in such a short period of time. Others slept, scattered around the floor, so that they would be fresh for more discussion the following morning.

Over the next few days there was a remarkable change in each of the six overnight recruits. Mike was forced to acknowledge not only the existence of God, but also the role that God had been playing in all that had happened in his life. Although Sheila had not been involved in a lesbian relationship for many years, she had defended homosexuality all her life. Now she had to admit that her stubborn prejudices on the subject had been no better than the prejudices that she had fought against. Her pride had blinded her to God's right to set standards with regard to sexual behaviour; but when she and Mike each broke down and acknowledged their stubbornness, it opened up new horizons for both of them spiritually, and it dramatically deepened their relationship with God and with the others in the newly formed community.

These transitions for Mike and Sheila were both traumatic and dramatic. But John, Luis, and Matthew each faced even greater struggles with their conservative religious hang-ups. Rayford's mention of a similar meeting with Hindus and Muslims was almost more than they could take.

The battle for them was one of fear. They feared that they were being lured into a heretical deception. Each one struggled in their own way. Matthew had been poisoned against The Family, as well as Jehovah's Witnesses, and John had been poisoned against all of "Christendom" as the Watchtower people called everyone apart from Jehovah's Witnesses. All three had problems with accepting the other, less fundamental, members of the newly formed union. Occasionally, one or more of them would take time out to escape in prayer, asking God for protection, strength, and finally for grace enough to lay down their prejudices and to fully embrace the evident sincerity, if not the truth, that existed in each of the others.

Sister Mary Teresa was caught in the middle. She had learned to tolerate, love, and appreciate people from many religious backgrounds. But she did so from what she confidently believed was a position of religious superiority. She had always thought that God would one day unite the world under the banner of the Roman Catholic Church. The Church had been her life and her hope. But now she was being forced to see it as just one more counterfeit in a world full of religious mirages.

When the six tribal judges-in-training were not sharing with and learning from each other, they were hungrily reading Rayford's writings. So much that he said contradicted a lifetime of religious tradition. But when they weighed it up against the teachings of Jesus and what they had been learning from each other, there was no denying both the validity and the relevance of it.

Ironically, it was Mike who had the least difficulty in accepting what Rayford said. He accepted it not because Jesus said it, but because he could see how it *worked*... to discipline people to be more spiritual and less religious. Motivations of greed and religious pride were replaced with a genuine hunger for more love and more truth.

They each came to see that this was what they needed to look for in others, and not religious or political tags. Sincerity could be found almost anywhere, and they needed to learn how to recognise it if they were going to be the leaders that God needed to unite all true believers in these last days. Rayford's writings had much to say that would help them along those lines.

By the end of the week, this new team was beginning to experience a miraculous love for each other, and they were discussing their next step.

Email and snail mail had increased significantly. The strange thing was that less than a third of it was coming from the United Kingdom. Dozens of people from Africa, South America, Europe, and the Middle East wrote in, asking for personal contact with the Jesans, as well as declaring their commitment to the teachings of Jesus as their standard for behaviour.

The original Jesans returned from an outreach on the weekend, and Neville and Mary returned about the same time. They too shared in the excitement of what was happening.

Because of their practical experience in living by faith, Rayford assigned each of the Jesan distributors to assist one of the judges in learning how to survive, both spiritually and physically in an alien world. Over the next three weeks, each of the new converts sold their possessions, giving the community more wealth than it had ever had before. From those funds air tickets and laptop computers were purchased for the newly ordained missionaries.

Sincere seekers were waiting to meet them in six different locations. Luis and Fran flew to Sao Paulo, Brazil. Mike and Martin flew to Ankara, Turkey. Chloe and Sister Mary Teresa took one of the vans on a ferry to France, and then on to Rome. Sheila had lived in Moscow for a few years when she was younger, so she and Reinhard (who also knew Russian) took responsibility for the work in Russia. And even young Raymie, who was now fifteen years old, was assigned to assist John Doorman in Johannesburg. Matthew Baker stayed in London to work with Rayford and Irene.

The tiny community was suddenly coming of age. "It's happening, isn't it?" Fran said when he first heard about the six new members. "It's coming together. Thank you, *Jeezus!*" And Fran gave high fives to the men who had been travelling with him. Chloe, Raymie, and the others just looked on and laughed.

Rayford addressed the expanded community before they all headed off to their respective destinations, one month after they had first met:

"You each will be responsible for almost half a billion people," he said. "You have just six months to locate 12,000 genuine believers from each of your tribal territories. You'll need to teach them as I have been trying to teach you. The notebooks will help, but they must be translated into local languages and reproduced as quickly as possible. You will face the same prejudices and closed minds that you yourselves had a few weeks ago. Pray for wisdom and patience, because you'll need a lot of it.

"But take heart... God *is* with you!"

Though awed by the task before them, they each felt Rayford's confidence as their own: God really was with them, and that was all that mattered.

Zion Ben-Jonah Writes

It is traditional to think of the twelve tribes mentioned in the Revelation as being flesh Jews. But we forget that the Jews as we know them today were only ever one tribe themselves (the tribe of Judah). The other tribes of Israel were wiped out even before Jesus was born. (Note: Even the names of the tribes in The Revelation are different from those of the Old Testament. Compare Exodus 1:2-7 with Revelation 7:4-8 and you will see that the tribe of Dan has been replaced by the tribe of Manasseh.)

What the twelve tribes of prophecy represent are "God's people". His people are not, by any stretch of the imagination, those who have rejected his Son. His people are those who have accepted his Son... those who follow Jesus (the Lamb) humbly wherever he leads, just like the Bible says. (Revelation 14:3-4)

Institutional Christianity's obsession with the Jewish race is a reflection of her own rejection of the message that Jesus came to deliver. God's goal is not to build a nation of people who possess Abraham's genes, but rather to build a nation of people who possess Abraham's faith.

The Revelation refers most consistently to Jesus as "The Lamb", in order to contrast his followers with those who seek a Temple made with hands (Acts 7:48) in which to sacrifice other lambs. Spiritual Jews have no need of a visible temple, while flesh Jews have no higher hope.

11. Soul Harvest

"Six months! It's not much time to reach half a billion people, is it?"

John Doorman was talking to Raymie Strait as they winged their way from London to Johannesburg, in South Africa.

But Raymie's head was a cauldron of other thoughts and emotions at that particular moment.

His mother -- *Irene* as he now called her -- had not taken his departure well. She didn't think he was ready for such a task; but *Rayford*... (Raymie liked the idea of his parents being spiritual brother and sister now.) Rayford had defended Raymie, reminding Irene of how much the boy had matured in the past year and a half.

Raymie felt sad for Irene. He knew that he still secretly felt like the little boy that she imagined him to be. But he was also thrilled about being trusted by his father with so much responsibility at such a young age, and he wanted to prove himself worthy of it.

Here he was, only fifteen years old, and acting as technical advisor to one of the world's twelve tribal judges. Who could have believed that the spoiled little brat who whined at the slightest inconvenience prior to the collapse of America was now an important leader in a worldwide religious movement!

Rayford's words came back to him. "You can do it, Raymie, as long as you remember each step of the way that you *can't* do it... not without God's help."

"Help me to remember that," he prayed for about the hundredth time since he had been designated to travel with John.

John Doorman had never had children of his own. He had never even been married. But he liked Raymie, and he showed a genuine concern for the boy's welfare. That was one of the factors that prompted Rayford to release Raymie into John's care. Together John and Raymie had been given the task of finding 12,000 genuine believers in the countries that made up Southern Africa and West Africa.

John's comment, echoing inside Raymie's subconscious, finally caught up with him, and Raymie responded.

"Yeah. It *is* a very big job, isn't it?" he said. "But we can do it, remember? We can do it if we just remember that we *can't* do it without God's help."

John nodded agreement, paused for a moment to ponder the truth in what Raymie had just said, and then went on:

"I have some ideas, Raymie," he said, pulling a small notebook out of his shirt pocket. "I want to get your thoughts on them."

One of the things that Raymie liked most about John was that he treated him like an adult, at least when it came to spiritual matters. Since John had learned to listen to others, he regarded Raymie as he did the other members of the Twelve Tribes, as a spiritual brother.

John's plan, as he explained it to Raymie, was to set up four separate bases in Johannesburg, one for translators, one for teaching, one for printing and distribution, and finally, an administrative and communication centre where he and Raymie would work.

"Sounds good to me," Raymie said.

"But it could take us six months just to train our first set of workers," the former Jehovah's Witness missionary lamented. "And we'll need *hundreds* of teams like that before we're finished."

"Remember what Dad... I mean, what Rayford said about us just being judges?" Raymie asked. "I think it means that we don't really have to teach everyone. God'll teach them if we just sorta make ourselves available."

Raymie patted the briefcase he was still holding in his lap. In it were the studies that Rayford had sent with each of the six teams.

"There's a lotta good teaching in here about listening to God, and about listening to one another. You 'member how you guys learned so fast from each other when you stopped being religious? We just gotta get *them* to do that too."

John didn't want to say anything to discourage Raymie, but unless he could duplicate Rayford's "big bang", as the group had come to call the explosion in Neville's lounge room, he was doubtful about his ability to get people to "stop being religious" as Raymie so aptly put it. He too whispered a prayer under his breath.

They were met at the airport by two married couples and two single men. Moses and Rebecca Mhlongo were in their late twenties, and had two small children, six-year-old Lebo, and Miriam, who was just over a year old. Ringo and Sylvia Laka were a middle-aged couple from Nigeria, but they had travelled to Johannesburg to link up with the others. Abdullah Ibrahim and Marcus Pietersen were both single, both from Johannesburg, and both in their early thirties. Only Marcus was of European descent. The others were all native Africans, and each had some knowledge of at least one native language.

When everyone had been introduced, and a few comments had been made about the flight from London, they climbed into two vehicles for the half hour drive to the communal apartment where they were all living.

On the way, John and Raymie learned that all six of the new recruits to their tribe (the tribe of Manasseh) had sold their possessions and put their wealth into a common purse. They had just moved into the three-bedroom apartment, which Abdullah, a government scientist until a few weeks ago, had previously been living in on his own.

John was keen to get started, so when they arrived, he launched straight into a business meeting, starting with questions about how the believers, who represented several different denominational and religious backgrounds, were dealing with their differences.

"Some problems were there on starting," confessed Abdullah in a strong Indian accent. "We were seven at first, but one woman was going when things were not as she wanted. Allah showed that we too would end up like her if we did not learn to listen to one another; so that is what we did. We simply listened."

John looked over at Raymie, who just smiled knowingly. "Well, thank God for that," he said. "Now if we can just find 11,992 *more* recruits like you people in the next six months!"

Rayford had concluded that the Temple in Jerusalem was going to take 220 days to complete, and he believed that it would take an equal period of time for each of the Twelve Tribes to come together as well. The others listened intently as John explained this theory to them, and they too were overwhelmed with the task that had been set out for them.

John then went on to explain his plan for four bases in each major city.

Fortunately there was more than enough cash from what each had received for their possessions, to rent four apartments, buy a truck, and get the presses rolling on literature. It was agreed that the apartment already being used by the local team would become the administrative headquarters, where John and Raymie would live and work.

Abdullah and Marcus volunteered to start immediately with translating. Between them they knew two tribal languages, Afrikaans and Arabic.

If they should need a rest, or if they were needed elsewhere, there were others in the team who could do translations in still more local languages.

Moses, who had been previously appointed as the group's accountant, agreed to locate and rent three more buildings, and to place orders for literature in English straight away, while print-outs in other languages were being prepared.

Ringo produced a notebook with the names of contacts the team had already made before John and Raymie had arrived. He and his wife, Sylvia, took upon themselves the responsibility of inviting these contacts to move into the education centre (as soon as they had one) and to start learning the ways of life within the Twelve Tribes.

Sylvia reminded them that the woman who had left had threatened to make trouble for the group. She asked how they would protect themselves from recriminations if other members backslid and turned bitter.

"Apart from leaders, there is no need for people at one base to have informations on other bases," Abdullah said. "We can work in cells. For members and leaders, other names will be used. That way, even if they are tortured, they will simply not be *able* to give informations."

Again John and Raymie exchanged glances as they observed how they themselves were little more than catalysts for something that was running of its own steam... well, at least of God's own steam.

Within two weeks, all four spheres of operation were up and running. Four others had moved into the teaching centre, where Ringo and Sylvia were acting as instructors. One of the new recruits possessed knowledge of yet another tribal language that the others did not know, and so she had been designated to join the translation team as soon as she had finished the basic training course.

Master copies of audio compact discs and printouts of key articles by Rayford were already being produced at the translation centre by the end of the second week. That is when the first order of literature arrived at the distribution centre. An order for another print run, this one in Afrikaans, was placed, and it was due for delivery the following week. Moses was now out shopping for a four-wheel drive vehicle to be used to deliver the literature to more remote areas... as soon as a new recruit could be trained to do that.

In a matter of weeks, the whole process would be repeated in places like Accra, Capetown, Harare, Monrovia, Kinshasa, and Lagos.

It was Raymie's job to answer the mail, and he was already receiving letters from people in South Africa who had heard of the Jesan website, and who wanted to adopt their lifestyle.

It was also Raymie's job to keep Rayford informed in England of what was happening. His regular epistles served the double purpose of putting Irene's mind at ease about his welfare.

What was happening in Johannesburg and beyond was not unlike what was happening in other cities where tribal judges had landed. Rayford had made contact with his counterpart in the Eastern Hemisphere, a man named Chaim Rosenberg, who was based in Sydney, Australia. Chaim was in his sixties, and he too had commissioned six judges. They were to cover all of Asia and Micronesia. The six Eastern judges were based in Sydney, Tokyo, New Delhi, Karachi, Beijing, and Hong Kong.

Over the next six months, the number of members in each of the tribes increased roughly three-fold every month. They worked quietly, trying not to arouse attention. The rest of the world was so intoxicated with a philosophy of love and peace at that time, that it was playing right into the hands of the Twelve Tribes. Even in countries where missionary activity had previously been outlawed, there were only cursory attempts to stop them when they pasted up posters in the middle of the night, or when they undertook other activities to alert believers to what God was doing.

But, although the doors were open, not many were walking through. They still only managed to find about one soul in 50,000 who was prepared to meet their standards. What they were fashioning was obviously going to be an elite team of spiritual commandos, who would be able to give godly leadership to the world, in what would soon become the darkest period in earth's history.

Zion Ben-Jonah Writes

Rayford's calculations were based on two passages from the book of Daniel, in the Old Testament. One predicts a period of seven years between an <u>agreement</u> that results in sacrifices resuming in Jerusalem and the "<u>consummation</u>" (or end). The other predicts a period of just 2300 days from the time the <u>sacrifices begin</u> until the sanctuary is first desecrated and then cleansed.

The difference between these two figures (2520 days and 2300 days) is presumably the time it will take to construct the Temple. (See box below.)

7 years (2520 days) left after the agreement (Dan. 9:27)

7	6	5	4	3	2	1

2300 days left from start of sacrifices (Dan. 8:13-14)

7	6	5	4	3	2	1

220 days: the time needed for construction.

Daniel 9:24-27 is so written that it could be referring to two parallel agreements, one between the prince of this world and his followers, and another between the Prince of peace and his followers. One results in a physical Temple being built, and the other results in a spiritual Body coming together miraculously.

But in either case, something horrible happens in the middle of the last seven years, resulting in an "abominable desolation" being inflicted upon both "temples".

12. The Temple

Mike and Martin were responsible for the Tribe of Judah, which covered all of the Middle East, as well as East Africa. When the Temple in Jerusalem was nearing completion, the pair made a rare trip away from their computers in Ankara to visit a tiny team of workers in the holy city. One reason for the trip was that they wanted to see for themselves what all the fuss was about. Mike's archaeological background included a keen interest in architecture as well.

The Pope had made good on his offer to move to Jerusalem, and a palatial residence was being built for him not far from the Temple Mount. The move was seen by experts to be on a par with Constantine's conversion to Christianity. By declaring Christianity the state religion, and himself the head of that religion, Constantine had lured early Christians out of the catacombs and into his courts, where they have been ever since. In a similar tactic, the Pope was now reaching out to embrace Jews and Muslims as "brothers" (whether they liked it or not); and in so doing, he was setting himself up as the unofficial patriarch of all three religions.

The Jews wanted their Temple badly enough to overlook such a move on the part of Rome; and the overwhelming presence of U.N. military might in Jerusalem at that time left Muslims with little choice but to go along with whatever their other two "brothers" had decreed.

Although 2,000 years of tradition had made Vatican City almost as sacred as the Pope himself, there could be no disputing the fact that Jerusalem outweighed Rome in the holy city stakes. The Vicar of Christ could not do better than to set up residence in the holiest of all holy cities.

In January of that year, the agreement had been made to build the twin temples. Now, some seven months later, construction was already nearing completion. Mike and Martin toured the site to observe the progress for themselves.

The Dome of the Rock, where Mohammed was said to have ascended into heaven, had been pretty much left untouched. This was possible because the Jewish Temple had been positioned in an East-West direction (rather than North-South) over the Dome of the Tablet, which was located just a few yards north of the Muslim mosque. The Temple entrance was perfectly aligned with the Golden Gate of the Eastern Wall. Following the original pattern for the Temple's construction (but using a slightly longer "cubit"), the new Temple fit perfectly on the northern end of the platform that had originally been built for visitors to the Dome of the Rock.

There was a matching *Catholic* basilica, called The Cathedral of the Divine Creation, built on the southern end of the Temple Mount. Outwardly it appeared to be a twin of the Jewish Temple; but the interior was laid out differently, in order to accommodate large crowds for mass, and a cathedral choir. Where the "holy of holies" was located in the Jewish floor plan, there was a Catholic *tabernacle*, to hold the blessed sacrament.

The entire platform area had been enlarged, so that there was plenty of courtyard space for the Temple, the Mosque, and the Cathedral. The two Christians could not deny that the golden Dome in the middle of two pure white matching temples was a masterpiece of religious architecture.

Religious leaders were abuzz with talk of how Jerusalem ("the city of peace") was finally going to live up to its name. The matching temples were a sure omen that world peace was on its way.

Prefabricated sections had appeared for the Temple, as if out of nowhere, reducing the time needed for construction. There was no waiting for materials or fittings either, as they had almost all been purchased or fashioned in advance and been stored nearby.

Much of the secular world did not care much about the Temple one way or the other; but there were some to whom it meant a great deal. Most surprising amongst this group, however, was Secretary General Xu Dangchao, a man who had never been known to show any religious interest in the past. He had cancelled more important appointments in order to be in Jerusalem when key decisions were being made about the Temple project.

While Mike and Martin were in Jerusalem a report came out in *Time* magazine (now based in Hong Kong) about Dangchao's ancestry. It was not given prominence in the magazine, but it did offer an explanation for Dangchao's interest in the Temple which Mike, in particular, was drawn to.

It seemed that, although Dangchao had been born and raised in Tibet, his parents had actually come from Kaifeng Province in China. *Xu* was one of seven Chinese names that had been adopted by some wandering Jews who had settled in China more than a thousand years earlier. The Jewish men had married Chinese women for so many generations, that their descendants were not racially distinguishable from their full-blooded Chinese neighbours. Nevertheless, because Chinese genealogy is so important, and because ancestral roots are traced through the father, the Xus of Kaifeng never forgot that they were Jews.

Few, if any, of the accessories of Judaism remained. But Dangchao's father had left one reminder of his roots. He named his son *Levi* Xu Dangchao.

The use of a third name in China was not unusual; but a *Jewish* third name was almost unheard of... outside of Kaifeng Province. Young Xu Dangchao had ceased to use his Jewish name when he moved from Tibet to England to study at Oxford University; and the question of him having another name had never been brought up after that, until now.

The news report suggested that Dangchao's Jewish ancestry was the reason for his keen interest in getting a Temple built in Jerusalem. Obviously, it said, he was showing loyalty to his ancestors, which touched the hearts of many. Of course, that did not explain why Dangchao was also instrumental in getting the Cathedral of the Divine Creation built on the Temple Mount.

Mike sensed something far more sinister, both in Xu Dangchao's third name, and in the three Temples. When he had read the story, he went back and studied Dangchao's full name, counting the value of the letters in it.

"There it is!" he said to Martin, who had read the article with him. "The missing numbers in his name. Add them up *now*, and see what you get!"

Mike was talking about the letters L, V, and I in the name *Levi*. They represent 50, 5, and 1 in Roman numerals. Together with the Roman numerals X, D, and C from the name *Xu Dangchao*, which represent 10, 500, and 100 in Roman numerals, the numeric value of his name came to 666; the predicted number for the name of the world's final global leader... the Antichrist. Mike knew Rayford had been pondering the significance of Dangchao's name, and so he passed the article on to him.

Rayford responded with a prediction to the Twelve Tribes: "In less than three years," he said, "Dangchao will cause the sacrifices to cease, and he himself will take control of the Temple. Of *course* he's interested in every detail of its construction. It will one day be his throne, and he will be demanding that the whole world worship him."

Rayford had written previously regarding what he saw as significant about the Temples themselves.

"They are a clever counterfeit," he had said, quite frankly. "They represent mankind's belief that peace can be found through the works of their own hands, and not through humble faith in God.

"It all seems harmless enough to people who have never taken *Jesus* seriously. Most of the church is still living in the Old Testament, where Temple worship was acceptable. So a building, even a complex of three different buildings, which unites three of the most powerful religions on earth must, in their eyes, be a good thing. But that's only because they recognise faith through buildings, and not through personal conviction."

The coming together of the institutional church was, according to Rayford, a diabolical imitation of the coming together of the invisible church, as was happening in the formation of the Twelve Tribes. World religions placed their hopes in political solutions, he said, while true believers were in tune with the Spirit of God, who would bring them together in his own way.

"Except the Lord build the house, they labour in vain who build it," he quoted from the Old Testament.

Mike and Martin were back in Ankara when the official opening came. But they watched live coverage on TV, along with the rest of the world.

* * *

The Cathedral of the Divine Creation was not quite finished when it came time for the opening of the Temple, on a hot summer day near the end of July. The media was not bothered by what was or was not happening with the Cathedral, however. They could see cathedrals any day, and almost anywhere. Their interest was the Temple.

There could only be one Jewish Temple.

Although the high priestly tribe of Levi had long since died out, a new tribe of priests had been artificially produced by raising selected Jewish boys under a strict priestly code of discipline. From these, a high priest had been chosen to preside over the affairs of the Temple, including its high profile opening.

Prominent Jewish religious leaders were present, along with many Jewish political personalities. Although non-Jews were not allowed inside, photos and drawings of the interior were given to the Press. Solomon himself would have been impressed. Almost everything was solid gold or silver, or at least gold or silver plated. Plush carpets, a closed circuit security system, air-conditioning, and a top class sound system all represented improvements on either of the two earlier Temples -- the one built by Solomon, or the later one built by Zerubbabel.

The first two Temples had featured the Ark of the Covenant, a sacred box in which the original Ten Commandments and other holy relics were held. Only the high priest could enter the "holy of holies" where the Ark resided, and he could only do it once a year. When he did, he would have a rope tied around his waist, in the event that he should die while there. It was believed that, if there was unconfessed sin in his life, he would be struck dead by the presence of God.

The new Temple had nothing to compare with the original Ark or the original Ten Commandments. But it did have a veritable museum of Jewish artefacts, honouring their history, both in Old Testament times and in more recent times. The housing of these artefacts was not limited to the holy of holies. They were displayed throughout the Temple complex.

When Solomon dedicated the Temple, fire came down from heaven and consumed the sacrifice. That miraculous flame had been tended continuously after that, to keep it burning. But no one expected God to honour the new Temple with such a display of power; so other arrangements had been made, which were arguably more sensational in their own way. A remote controlled laser beam was triggered to strike in the centre of the altar, igniting a huge eternal flame, into which the sacrifices would be thrown.

Dignitary after dignitary came forward with speeches of hope and rejoicing for this obvious fulfilment of Israel's destiny as God's People. Sacrifices continued throughout the day and on into the night, as lesser dignitaries waited patiently for their opportunity to make up for almost 2,000 years without a proper sacrifice on their behalf or on behalf of their ancestors.

There were tears of joy, and partying throughout the city all that night. The Wailing Wall had turned into a wall of rejoicing, and much of the world rejoiced with the Jews, who had suffered so much over the centuries, and who were now back worshipping in their own Temple... or at least in one that U.N. Secretary General Levi Xu Dangchao had arranged for them to use for a while.

Zion Ben-Jonah Writes

The curtain over the holy of holies was super-naturally torn, from top to bottom (Matthew 27:50-51), at about the same time that Jesus Christ said, "It is finished," and died on the cross, nearly 2,000 years ago (John 19:30). Jesus had predicted the destruction of that Temple (Matthew 24:2), a prophecy which was fulfilled in 70 A.D.

Although there was a misunderstanding about what he actually said, the only charge that his accusers had been able to get more than one witness to agree on during his trial, was that Jesus had somehow threatened their precious Temple (Matthew 26:59-62). Certainly, what Jesus represented was far more important than the Temple (Matthew 12:6). He spoke of a time when unity would not be determined on the basis of where we worship, but rather on the basis of invisible inner traits, like sincerity and faith (John 4:21-24). Our bodies have now become the place where God resides (I Corinthians 3:16).

Modern Christianity has, however, returned to the hype and trappings of Old Testament temple worship, so that the institutional church today is little more than Judaism with a new coat of paint.

But talk of unity which is based primarily on political organisations and visible structures is always going to miss the mark. Talk of love without submission to the One who is Love will never be able to produce the goods when called upon to do so.

13. The Mark

Many of the European disciples who joined Mary Teresa's tribe (which also included North Africa), had considerable wealth, which could be shared, not only with the poorer members in Africa, but also with tribes in other parts of the Third World. But getting funds from one place to another was not easy.

Europe led the world in adopting "the Mark", a microchip implant that was gaining in popularity throughout the world, because of its efficiency. The Twelve Tribes, like the Jesans before them, were opposed to the use of credit cards, smartcards, and especially to using the Mark. This made commercial transactions difficult for all of the tribes, but especially for European members.

The position taken by the Twelve Tribes came from a prophecy and a curse which appear in the 13th and 14th chapters of The Revelation:

"He (the Antichrist) causes all, both small and great, rich and poor, free and bond, to receive a Mark in their right hand, or in their foreheads, so that no one might buy or sell, save he that had the Mark, or the name of the Beast, or the number of his name." (Revelation 13:15-16)

"If anyone worship the Beast and his image, and receive his Mark in their forehead, or in their hand, they shall drink of the wine of the wrath of God, which is poured out without mixture into the cup of his indignation; and they shall be tormented with fire and brimstone in the presence of the holy angels,

*and in the presence of the Lamb. The smoke of
their torment ascends up for ever and ever, and
they have no rest day nor night, who worship the
Beast and his image, and whoever receives the
Mark of his name." (Revelation 14:9-11)*

Without the Mark, it was difficult for Chloe or
Sister Mary, or anyone in their tribe to make the
simplest purchases. Rayford and Chaim did not
teach that credit cards or smart cards were necessarily wrong, but they taught that a true believer
would want to err on the side of being too cautious,
rather than making excuses to move closer and
closer to taking the Mark. The hard part was that
so much business had to be done outside the
generally accepted channels. Sister Mary became quite adept at dealing through the Black
Market, although it meant paying very high prices.

Although some evangelical Christians had, in
the past, promised to oppose the Mark when it
came in, as soon as it became clear that it was
going to cost them personally, they adopted other
arguments to justify using it, as they had done
previously with credit cards and smart cards. The
most common argument was to say that a loving
God would never punish anyone for ever and ever,
especially not for doing something so innocent as
buying and selling.

One line of reasoning said that Christians could
take the Mark without necessarily worshipping the
devil, and as long as they did not "sell their soul"
to the devil, the grace of God would compensate

for their treachery. In its purest form the argument stated that even if they *did* worship the Antichrist or sell their soul to the devil, providing they had said a magical prayer "asking Jesus into their hearts" before selling out, God would be *forced* to forgive them. The teaching had been used to justify greed, pride, lust, dishonesty, self-righteousness, and every other sin you could think of for many decades before the Mark came in, so it was only natural that it should be extended to take in that form of disobedience as well.

The Mark took a number of different forms. By far, the most popular was the tiny implant, just under the skin on the back of the right hand. Technology had succeeded in making a little biochip (or passive transponder) that was so small that it was almost microscopic. It contained a universal pin number which was unique for each bearer. With the Mark in place, a person's right hand could be waved in front of a scanner using low frequency radio waves to verify the number before funds were added to or subtracted from that person's bank account. This would be done each time they wanted to buy or sell something.

An alternative Mark was available for amputees or others who could not use their right hand for one reason or another. These people could have the microchip implanted under the skin of their forehead. They could then just put their *head* in front of the scanner to authorise sales and purchases.

The third alternative was for people who (usually because of their great wealth) feared someone might kill and skin them, in an attempt to locate their transponder. Authorities assured the public that this would be virtually impossible, because the implants were extremely difficult to retrieve after they had been injected, and because a scanner would recognise anyone with two implants and it would refuse to process them.

Nevertheless, if people insisted on not accepting the implant, then they had the option of having a visible tattoo on their hand to signify that they had been officially "Declared and Certified Legally Exempt from Verification Implant", which was abbreviated *DCLXVI*, or 666 in Roman numerals!

People choosing the tattoo were allowed to manually punch their pin number into scanning machines, as it had been done in the old days before the Mark.

The only other exception was Dangchao himself, who needed only to use his *name* as identification. He had neither a tattoo nor an implant.

Chloe and Mary Teresa found that, even with Europe's widespread use of the Mark, new members had each failed to accept the implant or the tattoo for one reason or another. For some it seemed merely coincidental, because they knew nothing about the spiritual significance of what had been happening in the banking world. These amazing coincidences deepened the movement's conviction that God had been intervening in each of their lives, to protect them from the Mark. Nevertheless, Rayford and Chaim were quick to educate all members on the seriousness of what was happening, and on their need to be prepared to die before they would *ever* accept the Mark.

A few recruits had credit cards and/or smart cards, and in some exceptional instances these were used to do business on a temporary basis. This was particularly true of the European bases. Wherever possible, however, transactions were done with cash. Credit cards and smart cards were gradually destroyed.

The banks had brought in measures which complicated things for people still dealing in large sums of money. Paying for airline tickets, rent, printing, vehicles, and even food and clothing with cash always led to delays, and sometimes forced the believers to pay higher than normal prices.

Rayford and Chaim urged the Twelve Tribes to prepare for when they would neither be able to use credit cards, smart cards, *nor* cash. Chloe had learned much from her year and a half with the original Jesans, and she prepared a study on how to survive without such aids. Her three-pronged plan for survival, was called "Beg, Barter, or Steal." Begging and stealing shocked some members until the terms were more fully explained.

"It's really religious pride that we're dealing with," Chloe wrote. "We're only talking about doing things like stealing thrown out food from supermarket trash cans, or asking farmers for permission to glean leftover fruit from previously harvested fields. The barrier holding us back is not that we are doing anything immoral. It's really just a simple case of pride:"

In England, Rayford had gone over the study with his top leaders, and then finished it up with a group outing to some of the Jesans' favourite supermarket bins in the West London area. Every leader was expected to take a turn at climbing into a bin and foraging for food or other useful items. When it came Irene's turn, she crept hesitantly off toward the back of an Aldi supermarket, while Rayford stood guard in the van just around the corner from her.

Irene, who had somehow escaped participating in such an activity while she and Rayford had operated from the flat in Guildford, was apprehensive. She first squeezed behind the big industrial bin, in order to get a foothold on the fence next to it, before climbing in.

But then, just as she was about to lift herself up, she saw movement inside the bin itself, and she froze. There in front of her was a withered old woman dressed in several layers of rags, whose hair was unkempt, and her face black with dirt. The two women stared at each other in shock.

But it was the filthy, bedraggled bag lady who spoke first.

"Irene!" she shouted in amazement, and then she recoiled almost immediately, as though from shame.

Irene was speechless. How did this strange, almost frightening woman know her name? And then she saw something in the woman's eyes which she recognised.

"Elaine? Is that you? *Elaine!*"

Irene leaned far into the bin to hug the poor woman, who had begun to cry, both from fear and from relief.

By the time Rayford came looking to see what was taking so long, Elaine had told most of her story. What had been missed was told and re-told back at the flat when the bin excursion had ended.

Elaine Billings had been able to use Tom and Betty's car and money to get fuel, and to drive herself and her husband on to Montana, from where they had left Irene in North Dakota; but Vernon had died from the effects of radiation, only a week after they had arrived.

Those pilgrims who had reached Montana had quickly broken into factions when it became clear that there was no Messiah to be found. A couple of deluded souls had tried to pass themselves off as Jesus, while others insisted that they only needed to give God more time, and their dreams would come true. On the whole, it was a sorry, disillusioned lot of pilgrims. Most, like Elaine, were torn between losing their faith altogether and struggling to rebuild it on the basis of different criteria. Many of them died there in Montana before rescue teams came by helicopter to take them out of the country several weeks later.

It may have been good luck or just poor management that had brought Elaine to England. She had come on the understanding that she had a cousin there who would take responsibility for her. But in the confusion of the time, the authorities (many of whom were volunteers) had done little to check out the background to her claim. When she arrived, Elaine discovered that her cousin, a penniless recluse, had died of a heart attack more than a year previously. She was all alone in a country whose charity was already stretched to near breaking point.

Elaine had made no effort to link up with or seek aid from any church or charity, choosing rather to work out her own salvation on the streets. Despite her shocking appearance and confused mental state, Elaine possessed a strength of character that had not only carried her through the past year and a half but had been partly borne out of the circumstances in which she had found herself.

Elaine quickly regained what sanity she had lost through her ordeal. Because they had both been through such similar spiritual pilgrimages, she and Irene became closer than any two sisters. Irene saw her new companion as a blessing from God in replacement for the son and daughter that she had farewelled a few months earlier. Elaine was warmly accepted into the Tribe of Joseph as part of the Guildford administrative team.

But back to Chloe's lessons on survival without the Mark... "Stealing" was a pastime that Elaine had become expert at, after a year and a half on the streets. She had a host of helpful tips about living out of bins and surviving on other throwouts. But she was also good at bartering. She had learned to pick up little treasures that she found, and then later trade them with the right people for food, clothing, and sometimes even a night's shelter (although she relied mostly on begging to get shelter).

Bartering was a handy way to circumvent the Mark, especially when members of the Twelve Tribes were forsaking possessions that they had no need for in their new lifestyle. In later years they would most often do this to get clothing and food. If they were prepared to take a big loss, there was always someone prepared to give them what they needed in a lop-sided swap.

Unfortunately, bartering did not work with large purchases like travel tickets and motor vehicles, because of the paperwork associated with it. Consequently, the Twelve Tribes were told by their spokesmen to brace for a time when they would have to live *without* such luxuries.

Technically, the believers had until three and a half years after the Temple agreement had been signed before they would be forced totally outside of the economic system; but in practice, the test had already begun, especially for those living in the affluent West.

The Jesans, and a few others like Elaine, who had been living outside the system prior to the agreement, were the recognised experts on how to survive in an alien world. They had benefited greatly from having rejected credit cards and smart cards -- both forerunners of the Mark.

"We do not need any more information about the Mark than what is found in the gospels," wrote Chaim Rosenberg, in Australia "The Mark is never mentioned there," he went on. "But there, in the teachings of Jesus, we are told to be like the flowers and to be like the birds, who do not have jobs, do not plant fields, and do not weave cloth. God feeds them, and he will feed us if we will put his work first. If only we had taken that more seriously decades ago, we would be so much more prepared for what is about to happen now."

Chaim taught that most of the suffering that would take place amongst believers during the approaching Great Tribulation would be the result of disobedience to the teachings of Jesus now.

"The Antichrist will not have to hunt us down," he said. "Those with shallow faith are already lining up to receive his Mark. Others, who are brave enough to refuse the Mark, will starve or freeze to death without any action on the part of the Antichrist himself. It will happen because they never learned how to hear from God and how to obey him from day to day. That's what *we* are learning now. But those who run away from such discipline now will pay dearly for it in the next few years."

Zion Ben-Jonah Writes:

The Mark of the Beast is so close to reality right now, that debates amongst those who deny it is fulfilment of Bible prophecy deal only with technicalities. No doubt there will be changes in such things as implant and scanner technology over the next few years, but not even the skeptics would deny that the business world is committed to eventually using a form of marketing technology that was predicted in The Revelation, nearly two thousand years ago. And the prophecy says that the technology comes from the Antichrist.

Considering the dire warning that the same prophecy gives about accepting the Mark, one would have to be virtually dead spiritually to continue with the materialistic lifestyle that so much of the world (including almost all churchgoers) continue to pursue and to take for granted today.

At the moment, for most of the West, it is not as though they would have to risk death in order to just "play it safe" and live as the early Christians did. There is abundant wealth in our society, and there are a host of safety nets to help anyone who might wish to experiment with a lifestyle which is more concerned with spiritual things than it is with getting a new wardrobe or a bigger car. But still they choose to reject the way of Jesus.

With or without the Mark, the world (again, including the churches) continues to put its faith in, and to spend its life working for, the tokens that they wrongly believe will buy them happiness.

14. Peace! Peace!

From the day that the Temple was opened, membership in the Twelve Tribes (which totalled 144,000) froze. Suddenly it was as difficult to win a new disciple as what it had been before the Temple agreement had been signed.

Both Rayford and Chaim were prepared for it. They switched their emphasis after the Temple opening from outreach to inreach. Bases gradually moved from paying rent to squatting in disused buildings; laptops were updated to models that would pick up email from public phone booths; and more time was spent on theory. During those first seven and a half months, few of the 144,000 members had been able to find time enough to read, much less digest, all the truth that was in the material that Chaim and Rayford had prepared. Now they could spend whole days studying and discussing what had been prepared specifically for them and for their place in history.

Translators completed the articles that they had not been able to finish earlier, and Neville and Rayford were able to update all of the studies on the internet, creating links for sites in virtually every major language. CDs and audio cassettes were prepared and stockpiled, along with hundreds of tons of printed literature.

The material itself was altered, in many cases, because what was going to be needed for the next great surge would be different to what had just taken place. Rayford explained it in an article called "The Seal and Beyond". He wrote:

"You people have been *sealed* or especially selected by God to be the force that he uses to proclaim his message to the entire world in the last three and a half years of church history.

"Don't be surprised that you cannot see some outward *evidence* of your seal. The seal itself is known only to God. But our miraculous coming together as a worldwide, visible force is the greatest proof that he has chosen us.

"It may be that God will bring in others to take the place of any of us who die or who turn away from following the Lamb. But apart from that, there will be no further growth in our numbers. You could say that our fate has been sealed. However, as you each must realise, we still have our free will. We can still choose to reject our calling and be lost. Do not be drawn into tempting God by believing the lie that he has no right to take away your inheritance (as he did with the Jews, and as he has done with the institutional church); for if you do, your place will most assuredly be given to someone else.

"Nevertheless, God, who knows the end from the beginning, must know that at least the majority of us will freely choose not to turn back. Similarly, he knows that the majority of those who have *not* been included in our numbers will *refuse* to turn to him, no matter what happens.

"What remains for us to do now is to point the way for great multitudes to escape the curse of the Antichrist. But, to do that will, to a large extent, actually *create* the Great Tribulation. I will explain:

"As you know, people are daily accepting the Mark of the Beast, and they are doing it by the millions. They have been told by their religious leaders that they could do it and then claim ignorance, or that they can make some demand upon God's grace when Jesus returns, and they will be saved. It will be our job to preach most strongly against that lie, at the same time that we actually do offer those billions who have accepted the Mark of the Beast one last hope of salvation."

The Twelve Tribes were shocked by Rayford's claim that there could be a means of salvation even after people had accepted the Mark; but Chaim backed him up in what he said.

They were not told, however, what form their message of salvation to the Marked ones would take. They were only told that it would be revealed to them after the final three and a half years had started. For now, they should teach as strongly as possible *against* such a hope.

The tribes had heard enough to do two things. For one thing, what they heard challenged each of them to ask God for reassurance that they had not been deceived. They were living in a time of great deception, as had been prophesied, and what Rayford and Chaim were saying sounded suspiciously like the lie of perverted grace that they had each been delivered from.

The other thing that the message had done was to purify their attitude toward others who had taken the Mark. It was so easy to be self-righteous if, in fact, there was no further need to love these eternally damned people. But what if the world was not yet eternally damned? And what if the 144,000 themselves *could* be eternally damned? Such *doubt* about their own salvation and about the hopelessness of others was good for them; it worked against their natural tendency toward religious pride.

In the meantime, while the Twelve Tribes waited for the day to come when the message of salvation would be preached to the damned, it was hard to believe that they were actually living in the last days. The world had miraculously recovered from the greatest disaster in recorded history, as people put behind them the tragedy of more than thirty-five million deaths in America's collapse. On the heels of that horrible event, the rest of the world was, in fact, prospering as it had never done before. Xu Dangchao's incredible leadership had brought in a number of changes, each of which had benefited virtually everyone. Even the Twelve Tribes themselves had benefited from the new era of religious tolerance.

How hard it was to believe that the future held pain and suffering in store for the world, which would make the significance of the fall of America shrink by comparison!

"Use it! Use it!" Chaim had written in a list of instructions on how they should use their time during this period of apparent world peace. "But don't for a minute believe that it is genuine," he warned.

Chaim and Rayford both believed the authorities must have taken notice of their little movement by now, and they knew that it would just be a matter of time before the axe would fall.

A prophetic promise about God's people being given "the wings of an eagle," in order to escape the coming persecution, had stumped both of them. It obviously was poetic. They did not expect to sprout literal wings. But even if they had succeeded in gathering enough *aircraft* to fly themselves somewhere, they did not know of any place on earth where they could hide from the technology that would be available to the government to hunt them down.

Air travel itself was becoming increasingly more difficult, both because of the need for a Mark to purchase a ticket, and because of the number of authorities and regulations governing it.

Some Bible experts had taught that the place of hiding would be in Petra, a city carved out of solid rock, in Jordan. But it would hardly be impenetrable against modern technology, and if it was to have been secret, that cover had been blown by all the commentators who had announced it as the secret place in their writings.

Scripture called the place of refuge, "the wilderness", or "a desolate place", but neither of the two leaders could say where it would be. For the time being, they urged members of the movement to just maintain a low profile in their own localities, and to take comfort in the Rock of Ages, and in his teachings, which the Bible promised would be like a solid rock, protecting them from the coming "floods" and "storms". (Matthew 7:24-25)

Neville was joined by other computer experts who had become part of the Twelve Tribes, and together they had devised a series of satellite relays for their website which would make it difficult to track them down. But they still knew that it would only be a matter of time before that important link of communication would also be cut off.

* * *

It was less than three years since the Temple had been opened in Jerusalem. Half a dozen high level security experts were gathered in semi-darkness, around a series of sophisticated computers and other hardware in an office in Moscow, on a Monday evening in late June. Other office staff had gone home for the night.

One of the experts, a big man named Sergei, broke the silence as they all stood staring at the screen on one particular computer, obviously waiting for something to happen. "Any of you guys ever visit the site yourselves?" he asked innocently, in an effort to ease the boredom.

The others looked at each other, hesitant about answering. Sergei guessed that he had asked an embarrassing question, but he tried to patch the matter up with further talk.

"It's ridiculous, really. They think people can live without money. They say the implant comes from the Devil." And Sergei laughed nervously.

Still no response. The others turned and looked at Sergei, as though waiting for him to say more.

"I-I only checked it out because my son told me about it," he said defensively. But that put him in even deeper. Eyebrows raised, and Sergei's heart sank as he realised what he had done to his son by trying to excuse himself.

"Well, he didn't really... I mean..." he began, not certain how he would finish the sentence.

"There it is!" shouted one of the officers, whose eyes had returned to the monitor. Sergei, and his son, had been spared, at least for the moment.

"It's in England. West London!"

The men had succeeded in tracking down Rayford Strait's internet provider.

"We'll pull the plug on these traitors now!" said an older man, who appeared to be in charge. "But first we need to find out who's behind it. Oleg, get London on the phone!"

*   *   *

The staff at Web Wonders, in Clapham Junction, were just finishing up for the night, when it happened. The explosion came not from within, but from above, a powerful laser that cut straight through the building, and then exploded outward, totally reducing every thing and every one in that building to a pile of ashes, while, at the same time, leaving neighbouring buildings with little more than scorch marks on their walls. Web Wonders and all of their staff no longer existed.

The Great Tribulation was about to begin.

Zion Ben-Jonah Writes:

Many Bible commentators talk of <u>seven years</u> of great tribulation just before Jesus returns. But The Revelation is clear about there being two distinct halves to the final seven years. They are variously described as three and a half years, 42 months, or 1260 days. (Revelation 11:2-3, 12:6 & 14, 13:5, and Daniel 7:25, 9:27) It is only the second three and a half year period that is full of great trouble. The first half is what we call "the plastic peace".

While many have pointed to wars as the sign that the end of the world is near, Jesus actually said that wars are a sign that it is <u>not</u> near (Matthew 24:6). Rather, the scriptures warn that the Antichrist will gain spiritual control of the world through 'peace', or in some translations, through 'prosperity' (Daniel 8:23-25). The Apostle Paul, writing about the endtime, warned that 'sudden destruction' would follow a time when everyone was saying "Peace! Peace!" (I Thessalonians 5:3)

The Revelation also talks about an army of 144,000 faithful followers of the Lamb (Revelation 7:2-4, and 14:1-12), at the same time that it mentions a "great multitude which no one could number." (Revelation 7:9-17) This multitude is, in some way, brought to God during the period of Great Tribulation. Some believers are miraculously protected at that time (Revelation 12:14), but others are slaughtered in great numbers (Revelation 13:7). A puzzling paradox!

BOOK THREE
15. Assassins?

"I'd do it. No fear! I'd do it for God."

Neville was sharing his thoughts on an email which had arrived the day before from Mike, in Ankara. Mike said that the team in Jerusalem had passed within a hundred metres of Dangchao on a couple of occasions while doing business in the city. He said that security for the U.N. Secretary General was not what they had expected.

"He has guards with him," Mike wrote. "But if someone was prepared to rush him wearing a suicide bomb, I don't think they could stop him."

Mike's comments had sparked a debate at the Guildford headquarters about whether it would be morally right, knowing what they knew about Dangchao, to consider assassinating him.

"It's not like he's human," Neville explained. "If he's really the Devil, then what would be so wrong with killing him?"

Rayford was not there, but Matthew, as official judge for the Tribe of Joseph, spoke in opposition to Neville's theory.

"How do we know Dangchao isn't just as human as you or me at the moment?" he asked. "Besides, we're pacifists." The comment was significant, coming, as it was, from a former Baptist, who had always believed armies could be used to enforce the will of God. But that was before he had met the Jesans. "Christians don't kill their enemies," he said. "Vengeance is God's business, and not ours. Dangchao will get a deadly wound eventually, and maybe *that's* when the devil comes into him."

"Maybe we could be the ones to give him the deadly wound," suggested the older man. "We're supposed to fight for God at Armageddon. So if we can kill people for God then, why not now?"

"If you can kill Dangchao just by speaking a word, then go ahead," Matthew taunted. "But remember, Neville, that our weapon even at Armageddon is supposed to come out of our mouths. Our weapon is the truth... nothing more and nothing less. Do you understand?"

Irene, Mary, and Elaine listened intently, but said nothing. They were from the old school, where women listened submissively, in silence.

"Where do you suppose all the wars come from?" asked Matthew, pursuing his point a bit further.

"From greedy governments, fighting over oil and other wealth," Neville answered wisely. He had studied Rayford's teachings on the subject.

"Okay. True." That wasn't the answer Matthew had been looking for, so he offered it himself. "But they always get the soldiers to fight by *demonising* the opposition," he said. "If you can believe your opponent is sub-human, then you can feel justified in doing almost anything to him. But God doesn't work like that, Neville. He has his own ways of dealing with opponents."

The discussion ended abruptly when Rayford walked in with a newspaper in his hand.

"Heard the news?" he asked. Of course they hadn't, since it was Rayford's job to check headlines on a free paper at a local fast food restaurant each morning, and then report back to them if there was anything worth studying. But they sometimes tuned in to the BBC on the radio, and he was just checking on that before he spoke.

He tossed the paper down on the coffee table, where they could all see the eight-column headline:

Dangchao Killed

The report described how Dangchao had been stabbed by a spectator, while inspecting progress on a huge statue of Mary, the Queen of Heaven, that was being constructed in front of the Cathedral of the Divine Creation in Jerusalem. A three centimetre wound had pierced his heart.

"He was dead on arrival at Hadassah University Hospital," a spokesperson for the hospital had declared.

The news report discussed the identity and background of the assassin, who was killed by security men moments after the attack. It also speculated about who would take Dangchao's place. Tributes were rolling in from world leaders, who hailed Dangchao as one of the greatest leaders, if not *the* greatest leader that the world had ever known.

"Does that answer your question?" Matthew asked Neville, when they had recovered from the initial shock of the news. "If God wants someone bumped off, he can do it himself, without interference from us."

"So now what happens?" asked Neville. "Is he going to come back to life?"

"He will if he's the Antichrist," said Rayford. "We just have to wait. In the meantime, we need to pray about what *we're* supposed to be doing. Today marks 1,260 days since the agreement was signed."

The group spent all that morning in prayer and in serious discussion about where things were heading. They did not get any clear leading, and nothing seemed to be particularly different about the world around them. Had Rayford miscalculated?

They collected email from the other bases, and there was nothing significant happening there either.

Irene had business to tend to in London, so she caught the train into the city around lunch time. Late in the afternoon, she returned to the flat with a look of bewilderment on her face.

"Did you pick up email this morning?" she asked Rayford excitedly.

"Yeah. Why?" he responded.

"Have you picked it up *since* then?" she went on.

"'Bout an hour ago, I sent some stuff to Chaim and did a pick-up then," he answered. "Why?" Rayford's concern was not with Irene's question. It was with the sense of urgency in how she asked it.

"And did you have any problems?" she continued.

"What's this all about?" Rayford asked. "Is something wrong?"

Irene explained. "I stopped by Web Wonders, to make a payment on our account. There were police everywhere, but no Web Wonders."

"What do you mean, no Web Wonders?" Rayford asked.

"Nothing," said Irene. "No staff, no office, no *building*. Just a burnt out, empty block, with a lot of ashes and melted bricks."

"That's impossible. Are you sure you had the right place?" Rayford asked, as he moved toward the computer to try his email account once again.

"Sure I'm sure," said Irene. "I go there every month."

Neville had selected the tiny service provider because it was one of the few servers in the London area that still accepted cash. Irene could update their account by adding to their credit balance at the start of each month.

Rayford hit the right button to collect his email. "It's dialling up," he said, as they gathered around the computer, and listened to the familiar pattern of beeps.

"It's answering," Irene whispered in amazement. They listened as the screeks and squawks indicated that their computer was actually talking to Web Wonders' mainframe.

"Do they have another office somewhere?" Rayford asked.

"Not that I know of," Irene replied. "Mike's the owner, and he works there in the Clapham Junction office. I've never heard mention of any other office."

Just then, Neville drew their attention to the computer, which was now picking up their mail from the non-existent service provider!

"Look here!" he said, tapping the screen.

The program indicated that Rayford had more than 200 letters coming into his in-box.

"I just checked my box an hour ago!" Rayford exclaimed. "We've never had anywhere near that many, not even during the first six months." He was referring to the revival that they had experienced just after the Temple agreement had been signed.

"They're *real* too!" Neville explained. He caught glimpses of individual addresses flashing on the screen as each letter dropped into Rayford's in-box.

"But where are they coming from?" Rayford asked. "And what happened to Web Wonders? Do you think the authorities are on to us?"

The questions were rhetorical of course. No one in that room had any answers.

It took nearly half an hour to collect all of the mail, and while that was happening, Neville was considering how they could handle such large amounts of mail in future, if it continued to come in at that rate.

Rayford, on the other hand, was wondering whether they should run. According to all of their calculations, the Great Tribulation had begun. It was time for them to flee into the "wilderness". Whatever it was that had happened at Web Wonders, it was more than likely an indication that the authorities were on to them.

But where should they go? Where were the magic wings that would enable them to fly away from trouble? Or could it be that they were about to be captured? Had his ministry come to an end?

If it was going to end so soon, Rayford was determined to go down fighting. There was much that had been shared only amongst tribal members over the past three and a half years. But now it was time to broadcast it to the rest of the world... *if* he could still be heard.

Late that night, he sat in front of the computer, typing. He let loose with a broadside that left no doubt about what he believed about Levi Xu Dangchao and his world government. Rayford explained about the number value of Dangchao's name, and he predicted that the charismatic leader would be resurrected shortly, but that what people would see would not be a human being. It would be a zombie... a dead body inhabited by the Devil himself.

He predicted that the sacrifices would cease, and that Dangchao would take control of the Temple, declaring himself to be immortal. The Pope would call on the people of the world to worship Dangchao as the Universal Messiah.

They were extreme claims, but Rayford felt that he had very little time left, and he wanted to be as clear as possible before his arrest. It could be his last message to the world, and even if he was wrong in some of the finer details, he had to get the important point across to those whom he could influence: i.e. that Dangchao was the Antichrist. No doubt about it. He was evil personified. Anyone who worshipped him was nothing short of a satanist, whether they wanted to face that fact or not.

Rayford's one concession was to send a copy of his article to Chaim for approval before uploading it onto the site. He asked Chaim to place it on his own site, so that it would still be available, in the event that he himself was captured or met the same fate as the Web Wonders staff. Chaim suggested a few changes, which Rayford made, and then the article was uploaded.

Neville, in the meantime, was looking at the long run. If there *was* another office for Web Wonders, and if mail was going to keep coming in at the rate that it was coming in at the moment, they would need some kind of an automated system of response. He started by composing a letter telling people that there was no need for them to have personal responses, that they could find all the information they needed just by checking out the website. The site would be updated daily for as long as it remained on the internet.

If people still wanted to contact the leaders of the Twelve Tribes, they would need to ask God to show them how to get their letters delivered. This, too, was a bit of a gamble, and Neville prayed that God would help him by letting the right people crack the code. Neville set it up so that mail to their address at Web Wonders would only get through if people typed a 7 as the first digit in the text of the letter, followed by a letter, which would direct them to one of the Twelve Tribes... providing it was one of the correct twelve letters. Actually there were only eleven correct letters. Two of the Tribes started with a *J*: Mike and Martin's (the tribe of Judah), and

Matthew and Rayford's (the tribe of Joseph). Genuine enquirers needed to type a *Ju* for Mike and Martin and a *Jo* for Rayford and Matthew.

Neville's form letter gave no clues as to what people needed to do to get through. If they did not know the pattern that he had programmed Rayford's email in-box to follow, their letter would simply not be delivered. It remained to be seen whether God would tell the right people what to type in. Neville's form letter directed people to that material on their website which specifically taught them how to hear from God.

Of course, no one knew whether mail would continue to come in at such a rate, or whether they would still be around to collect it if it did.

Because of the late night, Rayford and Neville slept in the next morning, while Matthew and Irene took charge. Irene turned on the radio to hear the news. Sure enough, the lead story was that Dangchao had "revived". Press releases from the U.N. hinted that earlier reports had been exaggerated, and stated that Dangchao had responded to treatment on arrival at Hadassah Hospital, and that he was almost totally recovered. A photo showed him being released from the hospital with not so much as a bandage to show for the ordeal.

At the same time, Dangchao announced that the breech in security which had allowed an assassin to get so close to him had indicated a need for further changes in the structure and emphasis of the United Nations. He declared Jerusalem to be under the official control of the U.N., and said that he would need to use the Temple as "temporary" headquarters for the world body, because it was the most secure place in the city. The world media supported the move, probably because of the shock that the "assassination" had caused around the world. But no one asked why the switch to Jerusalem was being made in the first place.

The Pope went on record as supporting the decision, stating that the world was moving closer to one faith, and it was right and proper for that faith to become a part of the one world government that the U.N. represented. Dangchao's presence in the Temple complex symbolised that unity, he said.

There were objections from some Jewish religious leaders; but, surprisingly, there were voices supporting the move as well. Dangchao, some were saying, was the long-awaited Messiah. He was, at least technically, Jewish; and he had already shown that he was capable of ushering in world peace. So it was only right that the "city of peace" should accommodate him. These same leaders expressed disappointment, however, that Dangchao was not prepared to recognise the role of their official high priest, in connection with his duties at the Temple.

For the Twelve Tribes, the focus was in a different direction. By lunchtime on Wednesday, they and their leaders were on full alert. The Great Tribulation had, indeed, begun; tribal security may well have been breached; and they still did not know where they were to go to hide.

Zion Ben-Jonah Writes:

Some people mistakenly believe that, at some time in the future, God is going to so totally overwhelm the world with evidence of his power that they will have little choice but to worship him. Unfortunately, real life is not like that. There is always room for doubt; and prophecy is no exception. Look at some Old Testament prophecies about Jesus. Even now, with 2,000 years of hindsight, it is not so crystal clear in places.

Most of the world may not even be _aware_ of what is happening in spiritual terms when the final events unfold before the return of Jesus. And even those most aware of what is happening will almost certainly find some aspects of prophecy difficult to understand, as has been indicated in this chapter. But that is when they must rely on their conscience.

What God wants are people who will trust him and serve him even when they do not have all the answers. That is what the 144,000 believers represent... one person in 50,000 who will do the right thing simply because it _is_ right, and not because they have been forced into action.

However, one thing we must _not_ do, is to meddle with events in such a way as to try to either fulfil or alter what has been prophesied. Prophecy needs no help, nor can it be altered. It is not that we do not have free will, but rather that prophecy merely reports what will happen as a _result_ of our free will.

16. Two Witnesses

On Thursday morning, Rayford decided to check out the scene at Web Wonders for himself. He caught a train to Clapham Junction and walked from the station to where he knew the Web Wonders office to be. Police were still milling around the site, although most of the rubble had been cleared away. A handful of spectators were present too, discussing what had happened. Rayford moved closer, to see what information he could pick up.

The on-lookers knew less than he did about what was going on. But, shortly after he had entered the scene, Rayford noticed one member of the public talking animatedly to a policeman. He did not want to stare directly at them, but it appeared that both the police officer and the spectator had turned in his direction, and that the concerned citizen was pointing at him. Rayford decided to play it safe. He turned to walk away.

"Hey! You there! Stop where you are!" Obviously Rayford was being addressed, but with his back turned, he pretended not to hear, and he kept on walking. Just then two more policemen appeared in front of him. He was trapped.

He turned around, and leaning forward, pointed at himself innocently, while forming the words "Are you talking to me?" with his mouth.

"Yes, we're talking to you, stupid!" one of the policemen said as he grabbed Rayford roughly from behind.

He was dragged over closer to the informer, whom Rayford now recognised as Noah, a former member of the Tribe of Joseph. Noah had left the group in anger after a dispute a year earlier. He had declared at the time that the group was a cult and that its leaders were too authoritarian. Rayford had only seen Noah on an anonymous visit to Liverpool's distribution centre, where the man had been stationed. The centre had later been moved, and that was the last they had heard of, or from, Noah... until now.

"Yeah, that's him!" Noah said.

"I don't know what you're talking about," Rayford said, playing innocent.

"Do you have any identification?" the police officer asked.

"No, I'm afraid I don't," Rayford said honestly. He made a point of not carrying identification on himself, for just such an occasion as this. At least they would not be able to locate Irene and the others if they did not know where he lived.

"Do you know anything about the bombing of this building?" the police officer asked.

"Me? No," Rayford answered, genuinely surprised by the question. Why were they asking *him* about the bomb, when *they* were obviously the ones behind it?

"I'm going to have to take you down to the station for questioning," the police officer said.

"Am I being charged?" Rayford asked.

"Not unless you wanna be difficult."

"I don't understand. What would *I* know about whatever happened here?" he asked.

"Six people died when this building was bombed three nights ago. We have reason to believe that you know something about the bombing. Have you got something to hide?"

This was incredible. Did the authorities really believe that *Rayford Strait* had destroyed Web Wonders? Noah must have been brought in to watch for any believers to appear on the scene. And Rayford had walked straight into a trap.

There was so much that did not make sense. The police apparently did not have his address, which should have been on records at Web Wonders. And if there was another office elsewhere, they must not know about that either. Otherwise, they would have been able to access his files from there. Rayford himself was in big trouble, but at least the location of Neville and Mary's flat must not have been compromised.

"In the car, scumbag!" one of the policemen ordered, and he kneed Rayford in the back.

"Hey, take it easy!" he protested, as he fell to the ground and turned to rub his sore back.

"This isn't the movies, chum!" the policeman responded. "Just do as we tell you."

"NO!"

It happened again. But there had been no warning this time. Rayford did not even feel particularly angry. The word just came out of his mouth as he sat on the ground looking up.

As he spoke the word "No", a ball of fire reached out and enveloped all three police officers. This was far more serious than a flash of light and a few bruises on the victims, as had happened at Neville's.

Rayford could see that he was in big trouble if he didn't move quickly. As soon as the word was out of his mouth, he jumped up and ran. He was around the corner before the crowd realised what had happened, and even then they were not inclined to chase after a man who could breathe fire.

Two other policemen on the scene rushed to put out the flames on their partners, but it was too late. Three police officers had been killed by the mad bomber. Their partners did not want to be added to Rayford's list of victims; so they, too, did not pursue him. They phoned for help instead.

Rayford, in the meantime, had raced to the train station at Clapham Junction, and boarded a train back to Guildford. He was nervous all the way home, fearing that he may yet be being followed. He was also disturbed by what he had just done to the three police officers. And then there was the matter of the six people killed at Web Wonders. What was going on? Had he really played a part in their demise?

Subconsciously he knew part of the answer. He had known it for three and a half years now, although he had tried not to think about it. When others had tried to talk about it, he had always changed the subject.

"It's out of my hands," he would say. "I can't do it now, and so I'll just have to wait until I get to heaven for an explanation." He had been talking about the explosion that took place in Neville's living room three and a half years earlier.

The Bible taught that during the *final* three and a half years, there would be "Two Witnesses" who would be hunted by authorities around the world. These two prophets would have the ability to destroy their enemies through flames that come out of their mouths. Many people had aspired to be one of the Two Witnesses; but Rayford appeared to have the credentials that all of the others lacked. Three policemen were now dead on the streets of Clapham Junction as evidence of his authenticity.

When Rayford returned to the flat in Guildford, he brushed the others aside and went straight to the computer, where he sent a personal email to Chaim, marked "urgent". In it, he suggested that Chaim sever his links with his local service provider, and that he set up all of his mail to go through the Web Wonders connection.

With luck, the authorities had not yet located Chaim's server. If he cut his links in Australia, they would most likely not be able to trace him there. The two men would be putting all their eggs into one basket now, but it was a basket which had somehow been miraculously protected.

Either there was another Web Wonders office that had not been detected by the authorities, or else God had pulled some strings to set up an impenetrable website for the Twelve Tribes. Rayford was banking on the latter.

Then Rayford got to the real reason for his urgent email...

"I must know," he wrote, "whether you have had any experiences with fireworks happening when you speak. I mean literally. If you are who I think you are, you'll know what I'm talking about."

A few hours later, Rayford checked his mailbox again, and a reply was there.

"Yes, I have," it said. "So where do we go from here?"

Where *do* we go? thought Rayford. That was what he had been asking himself all week. But the list of questions was growing faster than any answers were coming in.

Nevertheless, if he and Chaim really were the Two Witnesses, then they were not likely to be captured immediately. According to the Bible, they had the best part of three and a half years left to make themselves heard around the world, and they may as well make the best of it.

The strange thing, as Rayford thought about it, was that so many people had aspired to play such a role (Mental hospitals were full of them.) and yet up close, the job of "endtime witness" had none of the glamour that others had so often associated with it. Already Rayford was being portrayed as a fire-breathing monster.

The scariest thing was that the description was so close to the truth.

Zion Ben-Jonah Writes

Reference to the "Two Witnesses," or two [endtime] prophets, can be found in Revelation 11:3-12. They have been compared with Elijah and Moses, in the Old Testament. Whoever they may turn out to be, they will certainly possess amazing powers, with which to certify their authority. The Revelation says that these two men will prophesy to the world for the final 1,260 days (three and a half years, or 42 months) of the final seven years before Jesus returns.

Because it is common for mentally unstable individuals to claim to be one of the "witnesses", most churches have shied away from any mention of the Two Witnesses at all. But the genuine should not need to give place to the counterfeit. With or without mental patients, there _will_ be two endtime prophets declaring the truth to the world.

It is significant, however, that there are _Two_ Witnesses, and that most pretenders to the role of endtime prophet operate independently... because their own delusions of grandeur make it impossible for them to submit to the counsel of others.

There is a biblical principle of everything spiritual being "confirmed in the mouth of two or three witnesses". (Matthew 18:16, II Corinthians 13:1, I Timothy 5:19, and Hebrews 10:29)

If it should happen that someone _must_ act entirely independently, however, then it seems that clear evidence of supernatural power may be regarded as a second "witness". (John 5:36)

17. Dangchao

Levi Xu Dangchao was discussing plans with Pope Pius XIII, who had only been in office for a little longer than Dangchao himself had been U.N. Secretary General. They were in the Pope's private residence in Jerusalem.

"The head is due to be placed on the statue in front of the cathedral tomorrow morning. Is that right?"

"Yes, it is," replied Pius. "It was cast yesterday, and it's being delivered today."

"I have a *different* head for it," Dangchao announced flatly.

"Another head?" the Pope asked in amazement. "What do you mean? Why do we need a different head?"

"What I *mean* is that I have had another head cast for the statue, and I want you to use it instead."

"But why? What's wrong with the one we had planned to use?"

"What's wrong with it?" Dangchao said to himself, as though searching for an answer. He looked out the window for a moment, to add a little drama to what was to follow, and then he said it again, sarcastically and slowly. "What's wrong with the head that Pius commissioned?"

He turned around slowly and faced Pope Pius. His face had changed. It was hideously contorted. And his voice was deep and raspy.

"What's wrong is that it isn't *me*!" he growled.

Pius drew back in fear. "Xu! What's happening to you?" he asked. "Your face...!"

Dangchao relaxed, and his face returned to its usual handsome calmness.

"Do you like this one better?" he asked.

"You scared me," said the Pope, relieved to see Dangchao return to normal.

"That was my intention," Dangchao replied. "A lot of people *trust* me, Pius. *You* trust me, don't you?" Pius nodded hesitantly, although he was not so sure anymore.

"But I would rather have you fear me," said Dangchao. "I would rather have them *all* fear me.

"And they will," he added as an afterthought.

Pius tried to swing things back to the original subject. "What does this have to do with the statue of the Blessed Virgin?" he asked.

Dangchao spoke softly, as though speaking to a child. "It has everything to do with the statue, Pius. You see, it's not going to *be* a statue of the Blessed Virgin. It's going to be a statue of me."

"I don't know if that would be appropriate," the Pope replied. The church had no problems with making statues of saints; and Dangchao might one day be honoured as such. But this particular statue was to be one of the biggest the church had ever made, and it was only right that the Queen of Heaven should be the one honoured, and not the Secretary General of the United Nations, even if he *was* widely regarded as the greatest leader the world had ever known.

"Do you want to see my other face again?" Dangchao asked, once more speaking down to the Pope, as though threatening a child. "You see, I'm not asking you. I'm telling you.

"You have your cathedral, as I promised, and you have your seat here in Jerusalem. But I expect to take *my* seat here too; and it will be as *I* say it should be."

Then, just for a moment, the hideous face reappeared. There was a cold chill in the room, and Pope Pius was overcome with a sense of fear that was so real he could almost reach out and touch it.

"*Do you understand?*" rumbled the creature that Dangchao had suddenly become.

"Yes... yes! I understand," Pius said, trembling in fear.

But he did *not* understand. And how would he ever explain it to the rest of the world?

"You'll see," said Dangchao, when the question had been asked, and when he was back to his normal self. "They'll accept it, just like you have accepted it. They may not *like* it, but they'll accept it. And they'll accept a lot more before we're finished."

Dangchao then proceeded to explain to the Pope what Pius' role was to be in the new regime.

"The chief purpose of religion has always been to enforce the legitimacy of the ruling powers," Dangchao explained. "And your role will be no different.

"The only thing that has changed in the present stage of evolution is that I am going to take off my mask. I'm tired of this hypocrisy. I want people to see me as I really am, and I want them to fear me."

It was slowly dawning on Pius that he was talking, face to face, with the one they called the Antichrist. The church had always played down such things. They did not like to worry the superstitious masses. But now Pius was being confronted by the real thing; and he had not been adequately equipped to deal with such an experience.

So he had been *tricked* into making the move to Jerusalem. He was there only for the purpose of propping up the rule of this evil man... if Dangchao really *was* a man.

But Pius could not go back to Rome now. And even if he tried, would Dangchao let him? He had experienced only a few seconds of the terror that Dangchao was able to inflict just through his presence, and he knew instinctively that this Beast was not going to turn loose of him easily. *He was Dangchao's slave*, and there was no way out.

He would watch for an opportunity to use his position to accomplish something good, of course; but for the time being, he had no choice. He must co-operate.

The new head arrived for the statue, and Pius was further disturbed to see that it was Dangchao's *hideous* face and not his real one. Or was the *hideous* face the real one?

Dangchao himself answered that question in another one of his patient classes with Pius later the following day.

"In order to get where I am today," he explained, "I have had to wear many masks. And all of them have at least appeared to be good people.

"But I'm *not* a nice person. I don't want people even thinking that I'm a nice person. I want them to fear me. I want to be able to control them. And I want to be able to do it without having to pretend to be nice.

"You see, Pius, that is the true test of power. Anyone can control people who trust them. But I want to be able to control people who *fear* me. You fear me, don't you?"

Pius had no choice but to contradict his earlier confession of faith in Dangchao and to nod in agreement with this new assessment of his relationship to the world ruler.

"Yes, you fear me," Dangchao said with a wicked smile. "You are even now looking for a way to escape. But there *is* none, is there? Where would you go? I control the world, and I am able to do it even when people like yourself would rather that I did not.

"I have been able to achieve that control through the Mark... through *my* Mark," he bragged.

Pope Pius looked puzzled, but he did not dare to voice his question. Nevertheless, Dangchao guessed what he was thinking.

"You question whether the Mark is truly mine?" he asked. "But that is because you continue to see the mask and you forget the reality behind it. Dangchao's face is not my face, Pius. You have seen the real me. Do I look like Dangchao? Of course not. I merely took advantage of his body.

"Oh, he co-operated beautifully with me before he died, as you yourself, and your predecessors before you, have done so often over the years. But it was only after his untimely death that I took total control of his body.

"But the Mark... I have been working on that for millennia. It is the symbol of mankind's dependence on me, and it is nearing completion. Yes, Pius, it's *my* mark, and I control the world with it."

Dangchao commanded the Pope to decree that the whole world should worship him, and that they should worship his image. The image of Mary in front of the Cathedral of the Divine Creation was to become the image of Dangchao, or rather the image of the Beast behind Dangchao.

"Don't be so sanctimonious," Dangchao argued, when Pius said it would be blasphemous. "You've been worshipping Mary for centuries, and she's far less divine than I am. The masses never complained about being told that Mary was God's Mother? So if you could get them to believe that whopper, why can't you just say that you've had a revelation that I'm God's Father?"

And at that, Dangchao broke into a fit of demonic laughter that chilled Pope Pius XIII to the bone.

Zion Ben-Jonah Writes

The Revelation talks about a 'Dragon' being cast out of heaven. (Revelation 12:7-9) The Dragon comes to earth, and makes war against the church, or "Bride" of Christ. (Revelation 12:12-13) This "Dragon" is, in fact, the Devil, who has come to make war against God and against all who believe in God. (Revelation 13:5)

The Dragon takes possession of a human body, which has received a "deadly wound". With the devil inside of him, this body is referred to as "the Beast". (Revelation 13:3)

The Beast is also assisted by a "False Prophet" (Revelation 16:13), who causes the whole world to worship the Beast and to worship the image that he has made of him. (Revelation 13:11-14)

Just as there will be a counterfeit Temple to parallel the spiritual temple that God occupies in the hearts of all true believers, there will also be a false prophet to rival the true prophets that God will send in the last days.

While true believers trust an invisible God to meet their needs, the counterfeit believers will worship a statue, and put their faith in the Mark (or money) to meet their needs. (Ephesians 5:5)

The most inspiring thing about the rise of the Antichrist, however, is that his hypocrisy will cease. People will be forced to take a stand, totally one way or the other. No more compromise, indecision, or double-mindedness. No more calling evil good and good evil! Thank God for that.

18. The Gospel

When he had recovered his composure, and was wiping away the tears that he had shed during his fit of laughter, Dangchao spoke once more to the Pope.

"I'm going to need your help with one other little matter," he said. "There's a religious cult that has been saying some nasty things about me and my government. We tried to track them down on the internet, but they destroyed the entire building where their provider was based, before we could get their address. They go by the name of Twelve Tribes. What information do you have on them?"

The church maintained extensive files on all new religious movements, in their offices in Rome; but why, thought Pius, should he help Dangchao? What if these people offered some hope of *stopping* this terrible man? If they did, then he should be helping *them* instead of helping Dangchao.

The General Secretary sighed deeply as he caught the drift of what Pius must be thinking. He would have to play the pious game himself once again, as he had done so often over the years, in order to control the Pope.

"Whatever you might think of me," he said kindly, "the facts are that this is a very dangerous cult. They've already killed nine people that we know of, and there is talk of others having been killed by one of them in Australia as well. Pius, Please! You would be doing the world a *service* if you could help us to stop them."

Pius thought for a moment and then decided that if he was going to be heroic, this might not be the best cause to support or the best time to act. But if he were to assist Dangchao this once, he might win his favour. Then he could use that favour to achieve a greater good at another more expedient time in the future.

Dangchao smiled to himself. The old charm never failed. Keep him procrastinating, and he would keep him under his control forever.

In a matter of an hour and a half, Pius had a complete report on the Twelve Tribes faxed through from Rome, but it was little help to either of them. Catholic researchers had a small file from the days of the Jesans, which included Reinhard's name. However, almost all of what they had on the Twelve Tribes movement since then had come from material that was already freely available on the Twelve Tribes web site.

Despite attempts by the Church's New Religious Movements Committee to woo the Jesans and then to woo the Twelve Tribes into giving them inside information, there had been no response from either Reinhard, Rayford, or Chaim. Even their names were unknown, because Rayford and Chaim always wrote anonymously. The committee had not found anything obviously dangerous in what they taught, and so they had not pursued the group further.

There were some who said the movement was huge, numbering in the millions; but there were more who believed it was an illusion, caused by a handful of people who wanted to give the impression that they were bigger than what they really were. After all, there were no buildings, no postal addresses, no record of meetings, and no names of either leaders or followers, apart from Reinhard and a few ex-members. It was true that they did produce a lot of literature, but even their literature gave only the web site as a contact address.

"We've put some of the world's best hackers on the job, and they've all hit dead ends," Dangchao lamented to Pius when he had finished reading the report from Rome. "Everything indicates that Web Wonders, their service provider, does not exist. And yet their web site continues to function. We seem to have no way of blocking it."

In fact, the Twelve Tribes hit counter was spinning wildly. And it increased in momentum over the next few months. Each time another media report on Dangchao came out, thousands more would visit the Twelve Tribes site to get an update from the Two Witnesses on what they had to say about what was really happening.

Had Dangchao overplayed his hand? The media did not know how to respond to reports that he was the Father of God, or any of the other outrageous things that he and Pope Pius were getting up to in Jerusalem.

The monstrous statue with its gargoyle head and female body, purporting to be a statue of Dangchao, shocked the world, but it was only the start of other shocks.

Dangchao ripped out the holy of holies from the Temple, and put a throne there for himself to sit on while being worshipped and admired by members of the public. He invited people of all religions and of no religion to come there to worship him, thus severing his relations with the Jewish leaders who had hoped that he might be their Messiah.

He insisted on providing entertainment for his visitors, and his choice of entertainment became more and more blatantly blasphemous. First it was music praising himself as the Saviour of the world, the Prince of Princes, and the Lord of Creation. Then the music started making fun of the real God. Dancers were brought in, who became more and more suggestive in their routines. Powerful drugs were freely dispensed to guests. In the space of just a few months, Dangchao had incorporated live sex acts and other far worse perversions into his system of worship within the Jewish Temple.

But the most surprising thing of all was that people were accepting it. Like he had predicted, even those who did not like what he was doing were so weakened morally that they were not able to resist him.

There were others who flocked to worship him, and to participate in his bacchanalian festivals, with obvious *enthusiasm*. It was quickly becoming the in-thing amongst diplomats and other highly respected people, to be seen at one of Dangchao's obscene celebrations.

It was even reported that during some of the most extreme activities conducted at the Temple, his whole appearance would magically change, and people could experience first-hand the awesome supernatural power that he possessed.

The media, although stunned, was powerless to do anything more than report what was happening, as if it was normal behaviour from a world ruler. Dangchao, who seemed capable of working all day and partying all night, had the banks and key members of the United Nations securely tucked in his pocket. Between the two institutions, he controlled the world, and no one dared challenge him.

Nevertheless, his public stand against God and his attempts to offend all sensibilities, were what caused so many hundreds of thousands of people to seek out the Twelve Tribes for counsel and explanation. There was no longer any doubt about where Dangchao was coming from. He was, indeed, the Antichrist, the personification of evil.

Word quickly spread around the world about the Twelve Tribes site. Its address was painted (under cover of darkness) on walls and hoardings wherever the faithful 144,000 believers could find a space to fill.

So, as people saw what was happening in Jerusalem, they would turn to Rayford and Chaim for explanations. In a very short time, literally millions of people were visiting the web site, which had become the official mouthpiece of God's two endtime Witnesses.

A few people had cracked Neville's email code
and they had been able to get letters straight
through to the tribes. These people were being
dealt with personally. Most of them had still not
received the Mark, and so they were quickly taken
into fellowship, on the assumption that God had
both protected them from taking the Mark and
been instrumental in helping them to work out the
email code. Based on this theory, such people did
not represent a security risk.

Between the email code and the anonymity of
the website, the 144,000 had, indeed, escaped
into a "wilderness" of safety from the authorities.
God himself controlled who would have access to
them, and the rest of the world was locked out.

With the exception of isolated individuals and
some of the most rural and primitive villages in the
Third world, virtually everyone on earth had received the Mark by this time. It was impossible to
do business without it. Those Twelve Tribe members who had not been successful in getting free
rent from personal friends in the system were
being forced out onto the streets, or into tents and
other makeshift accommodation. But overall they
were surviving without undue hardship, using the
principles of begging, bartering, and stealing the
most basic necessities of life in this insanely evil
new world order.

The people who were in the worst predicament
were the ones who were now visiting the Twelve
Tribes out of desperation. What they had read

about the curse on those who took the Mark had virtually put them into a hopeless situation spiritually. They were without any means of salvation, and they were living in a world that was growing rapidly more evil every day.

Dangchao brought back gladiatorial sports, the ultimate reality games, where contestants fought to the death. He had also arranged to televise public tortures and executions in Jerusalem as a form of entertainment. But many people who had never given God much thought before, were becoming sickened by it all, and they wanted out.

So Chaim and Rayford released the plan of salvation that they had hinted at in a previous message to the 144,000. It had become the lead article on the website, and it shocked the world.

Here is what it said:

"God's plan of salvation today is really no different to what it has always been. You need only accept Jesus Christ as God's Son, and as your only hope of salvation.

"The difference (for those who know something about what used to pass as Christianity) is that we are not talking about some cheap *pretence* at faith this time. Accepting Jesus means accepting everything that he has said. His teachings are a necessary part of God's plan of salvation for you. Read his teachings and you'll see that he expects *total* faith, and total obedience. His standards are high, but what he offers is eternal life. No price could be too high for that."

Rayford explained that his sacrificial death on the cross had bought Jesus the right to give salvation to whomever he chose; but it did not obligate Jesus to choose just anybody. He had certain standards that he was looking for first.

"Some of your religious leaders have taught that a loving God cannot set standards, make demands, or put a 'price' on what he offers," he said. "But where have they led you? They have brought you to the brink of hell. What they taught sounded like 'good news' at the time, because it was so cheap and easy. But it has turned into the worst possible disaster.

"In contrast, the gospel that Jesus preached really *is* good news, even if it is not cheap. It is good news because he could see what each of you have tried to ignore all your life. He could see your utter hopelessness. He could see that, with or without the events that are happening in the world today, you are going to die one day, and you are going to be punished for your failure to obey God. He knew that *whatever* price he might put on his plan of salvation, the price would be incidental by comparison to what he was offering... a total pardon, and eternal life in a world that is infinitely more beautiful and more satisfying than the one that we now live in.

"So what is the price that he asks? He asks that you forsake *all*, i.e. that you give up everything that you now have... your possessions, your livelihood, your family and friends, and even your own life.

Take it or leave it. That is his price. It has always been his price, and it still is his price. The offer is still open to you now. But there will be no cheating on the rules this time.

"Most of you who are reading this message have already accepted the Mark of the Beast, either in your right hand or in your forehead. Most of you also know that the Bible says that anyone who receives that Mark will experience the undiluted wrath of God, and that you will be tormented with fire and brimstone in the presence of Jesus and in the presence of his holy angels. You will be cast into the lake of fire, which burns forever and ever. These are real threats. You may not think that it is 'loving', but remember... *you* don't make the rules; God does. Until you accept that, you will never be able to discover just how loving he really is.

"Now here is what the good news of Jesus Christ means in practical terms for those of you who have already taken the Mark of the Beast. It means that you must cut off your right hand, or allow yourself to be beheaded for the sake of the gospel!

"That's right. Jesus said that if your right hand offends you, you should cut it off... that it would be better for you to enter into heaven without a hand, than to go to hell because of what your right hand represents. For years people have pointed to that very teaching of Jesus as proof that he never seriously meant for us to take him

literally. But now it is time for believers everywhere to prove their faith by their actions.

"Many of you never heard the warning about the
Mark of the Beast. But you did hear the voice of
God speaking to you through your own conscience,
and you rejected it. For one reason or another, you
chose to go your own way, to move gradually away
from the ideals of your youth and the ideals of your
various religions. And it is because of your insin-
cerity and double-mindedness at those times that
you have ended up where you are now.

"Remember, God is not asking anything of you
that he hasn't asked of everyone else. The difference is that we who are writing to you now... we
took the still, small voice of his spirit seriously
before accepting the Mark of the Beast, and we
refused to take it. We responded to God speaking
through our conscience as well as through his Son.

"Sure, we were inconvenienced, and even now
we are being inconvenienced for our decision to
put God first. But overall, we have come out
ahead. You who are reading this chose to delay
your decision, thinking it was too difficult or too
inconvenient to put God first, and you have brought
this situation upon yourselves as a result.

"We can conclude by telling you that the offer is
real. God is real. Heaven is real. Jesus really is
God's Son. And what he offers is genuine. Eternal
life. Eternal happiness. Eternal peace.

"But the full terms of the offer require you to turn
loose of your present life to get it. It's your choice."

Zion Ben-Jonah Writes

A number of theories are going around about ways that Christians can accept the Mark of the Beast and still escape punishment for doing so. They mostly centre around the "grace of God", and how a loving God would not punish anyone who says Lord, Lord to Jesus... whether or not they ever get around to even trying to obey him. But, of course, such a teaching is a _perversion_ of the grace of God, and it makes a mockery of all that the Bible (and Jesus in particular) say about obedience.

It may well be that merely _accepting_ the Mark (as the Revelation technically teaches) is enough to land one in the lake of fire eternally, without any hope at all. However, what Jesus said in the Sermon on the Mount about cutting off your hand if it offends you (Matthew 5:30) at least presents a sobering picture of what would be the terms of a gracious "second chance"... _if_ there is to be such a thing as a second chance.

The bottom line is that the longer one delays in obeying God, the harder it is going to be. Who knows for certain that there is not hope for repentance even in hell itself? But then who wants to go there to find out?

The Bible says, "Now is the accepted time. Today is the day of salvation. Today, if you hear his voice, do not harden your hearts as the Israelites did in the wilderness, thus provoking God's wrath." (II Corinthians 6:2, Hebrews 3:7-8, and Hebrews 3:15)

19. Tribulation Force

Fifteen tribal members crowded into the lounge room of the main teaching house in Sao Paulo. Furniture had been removed to make space for them, and for the large legless table-top that lay on the floor in the middle of the room. It had strong leather straps attached to it at each side.

Luis had arrived back from Rio that same morning. In Rio, he had watched a proper doctor do this only twice before he was given the task of operating on his own. Now, less than two weeks later, he was to teach others how to do it. There was a long waiting list in Sao Paulo, as more and more people were cracking the email code and begging for help to escape the Mark.

"You have two choices," Luis had said to his first patient earlier that day, while ten others had listened to the same speech. They had all been brought there blindfolded. "We can take the skin off the back, or we can take the whole hand. We're ninety percent certain of getting the transponder by taking the skin, but it *could* have worked its way down under the ligaments too."

"No, please, senor! Take it all off!" pleaded the patient, a poor farmer in his 40's, named Joaquin.

"The demons, they are everywhere," he continued. "I cannot sleep. I cannot think. Please take it all off. God, help me!" and his eyes looked heavenward.

Now Joaquin was being strapped to the contraption on the floor, like a prisoner on a cross.

The front door opened a crack, and Francisco peeked in. "I got 'em," he said, as he entered the room and closed the door behind him. He pulled a fistful of Stanley knives out of his sleeve. "Had to steal 'em. May God forgive me." His head dropped in a posture of repentance.

"I think that, under the circumstances, God will understand," Luis said comfortingly.

Fran raised his head and let a little grin escape. "I'm glad you see it that way, Luis," he said, "'cuz I didn't feel guilty at all when I took it. Felt kinda good, actually!"

The others smiled only slightly. The scene was far too tense for anything more frivolous than that.

Joaquin, who had been given a handful of pain killers to swallow ten minutes earlier, was firmly strapped in. Two men kneeled on the floor, straddling his legs. Two women moved closer to his head. They too were on their knees, but they were holding Bibles. They would take it in turns reading Psalms in Spanish, while Luis performed the operation.

When they were ready to start, a heavy piece of leather was placed in Joaquin's mouth, so that he could bite into it. It was important that they not arouse the suspicions of their neighbours, and because of that, Joaquin could not afford the luxury of screaming out his pain.

A ball of rags was placed in his left hand. He was instructed to hold his right hand as still as possible throughout the operation.

"The Lord is my shepherd. I shall not want," Felicidad began in Spanish. She continued to read softly as Joaquin focused intently on her words.

The first razor blade knife had been cleansed with alcohol. Luis applied a rough tourniquet, gripped Joaquin's lower arm to steady it, and then made his first cut, across the upturned palm, using the extendable razor. Joaquin's body tensed and he bit hard on the leather.

"Yea, though I walk through the valley of the shadow of death, I will fear no evil; for thou art with me," Felicidad continued. *"Thy rod and thy staff, they comfort me."*

"We need to allow for extra skin from the palm," Luis explained, as he grabbed a needle and thread to tie off an artery. "When we finish, we'll fold that skin over the stump, and join it to the upper portion."

Because he had no proper surgical clamps with which to grasp the end of a loose artery, Luis tied most of them off right through the skin, a short distance back from where he had made the cut. He used a simple pair of pliers to hold the skin if necessary. Deeper arteries needed to be cauterised with a hot piece of wire... a particularly painful procedure.

The tourniquet had reduced bleeding to a trickle, so that it was not easy to determine whether either the thread or the hot wire had done their job. Luis had a chart in front of him showing where to look for the major arteries.

"Very tight bandaging should take care of the smaller vessels," he said.

Joaquin's eyes were filled with tears, and the knuckles on his left hand were white from squeezing the rags. His whole body struggled in an effort not to move his right hand.

"Weeping may endure for a night, but joy cometh in the morning..." Maria read, while Felicidad looked for another suitable Psalm.

Luis made a sudden, forceful movement with the razor, and Joaquin's body lifted off the table. The two men struggled to hold him still. He whimpered quietly, and beads of perspiration ran down the sides of his head.

"There! We've cut through most of the nerves," the instructor was saying to his startled students.

"The hardest part is over now, Joaquin," he said softly to his patient.

Luis spoke less now, as he fully busied himself with what he was doing. His wide-eyed students crowded closer to watch.

It was Felicidad's turn to read when the operation was nearing completion. *"Blessed is he whose transgression is forgiven, whose sin is covered. Blessed in the man unto whom the Lord imputeth not iniquity, and in whose spirit there is no guile,"* she read.

Joaquin arched his neck back to look directly at Felicidad. Tears ran down his face, as much in response to the words he was hearing, as in response to the pain he was feeling.

All that was left now were some ligaments joining the bones of the wrist together. Luis pushed hard with the Stanley knife, to cut through the largest of the ligaments while missing the bones on either end of it.

Joaquin's eyes closed and he went limp. He had mercifully passed out.

When the procedure was finished, and Joaquin's stitched up stump was wrapped and bandaged, Luis reminded his audience that he would do only one more demonstration before they would have to perform the same operation on their own. They would each be expected to do one patient before the day had finished. And they would be doing many more in the days ahead.

He finished up with basic instructions on how to nurse the patient in the days after the operation.

The whole ordeal had emotionally drained all those involved; but even before the wound had begun to heal, when Joaquin was conscious once again, he smiled through his pain. His whole countenance had changed, and he glowed as he spoke of the peace he felt.

Luis warned him that there could still be complications. Infections were commonplace, and without antibiotics, a few amputees had already died from them.

"That is not a problem," said Joaquin. I am happy to die for my God now. My heart, it is free. Thank you, God! You know, brother, I am happy to die for Jesus now... *really* happy."

And Joaquin was not exceptional amongst those who came to have the Mark removed. All over the world a revolution of faith was taking place. People who had never taken seriously the demands of God were discovering peace, joy, love, and courage in the face of death, as they exercised obedience to this one command of Jesus. It had become the new rite of initiation into the ranks of the redeemed... a baptism into Christ's suffering. It represented a true circumcision of the heart, as they turned from the lie of false grace to genuine faith in Jesus Christ and all that he taught.

Unfortunately, this amputation of the Mark was only the start of the suffering for these people. Their missing hand became an inescapable testimony to the rest of the world of their stand against the Mark. Everywhere they went, people turned and stared... not just because they were different, but because the public was seeing more and more people with missing hands. Something was happening, and the most forward members of the public would stop the amputees to ask.

"How did you lose your hand? I have seen others like you. What does it mean?"

And from that, the message was being preached by word of mouth to any who had not yet visited the web site. Those who heard the testimonies of the amputees would pass it on as faithfully as they had received it, for there were none who were untouched by what they heard.

It was necessary to hide the amputees during their initial period of recovery. They were given as much teaching as possible during that period, and then they would be put in touch with other amputees in a separate location. They would be smuggled out of the safe houses blindfolded, under cover of darkness, to where they would begin their existence in exile, living like outcasts on the fringes of society. They knew that it would only be a matter of time before their obvious deformity would make them targets for arrest. But they had made their choice, and they all, like Joaquin, were happy to die, if necessary, for their new-found faith.

Because the Mark was invisible, the 144,000 of the Twelve Tribes looked no different to everyone else as they walked the streets. And because of this, they were able to stay anonymous throughout the final three and a half years.

But the amputees became the public image of the movement. They came to be referred to, amongst the believers, as the Tribulation Force. What Rayford and Chaim's two-dimensional testimony on the internet could not do (despite the powerful truths contained in it), a living testimony from the Tribulation Force made up for. These people who had made such a sacrifice and still boasted of the riches that they had received in return... as though their salvation had cost them nothing... were a powerful testimony to the true grace of God.

The Tribulation Force had no promise of refuge in the wilderness as did the 144,000. They believed that, as spiritual lepers, their days were numbered. It would not be long before Dangchao and his troops would round them up for execution, if Rayford and Chaim's understanding of prophecy was correct.

But knowing this only caused them to be more bold in preaching the good news of Jesus. They wanted to help others to escape from the curse that hung over the planet, and their positive glowing testimony was something the Twelve Tribes could not match. Thousands more were coming every day, to join their ranks. The world was receiving, through this new movement, a wake-up call to what it means to have real faith in the midst of a godless generation.

*   *   *

At the same time, there was a transformation of a different sort taking place in the halls of power in Jerusalem. Pope Pius, who had vowed to do something heroic "some day", was moving farther and farther away from the likelihood of such a move. He, who had convinced himself that it was not "possible" to take a stand against the Antichrist (because it would have threatened his position, his organisation, his reputation, and his comfort) had been shamed and angered by the testimony of the single-handed members of the Tribulation Force, whom he mistakenly assumed to be the hated Twelve Tribes.

Pius was able to forget about the real sins of Dangchao by concentrating on the perceived excesses of this group of fanatics, and the pain and suffering that he believed they were causing all over the world. His mission, with Dangchao, to track down the Twelve Tribes became more and more of an obsession, until he had convinced himself that his true calling in life was to protect the world from such obvious abuse of religion.

Living and working so close to Dangchao had the same effect on Pius as living next to a sewage treatment plant has on local residents. What shocks the senses of visitors ceases to be noticed at all by those who live around it day after day. Dangchao had his vices, it was true; but he was trying to bring stability to the world at a very difficult time. The stresses of his office had probably led him to act in the way that he did. The important thing, Pius told himself, as he cauterised his conscience, was to maintain the unity of the church, and the unity of the government. A few compromises along the way were unavoidable. They were part of the price he would have to pay for the times in which he lived.

Pius was talked into making secret alterations to the statue in front of the basilica. A speaker was installed, as well as a series of guns around the base of the statue. Great crowds gathered in the forecourt each day, and the giant image would "speak" to the crowds at random intervals, saying, "Bow down and worship your king and

your god!" Five seconds after the announce-
ment, the guns, which were placed about a metre
above the ground, would fire.

Scores of people were killed or injured the first
time that the guns went off. There had been no
warning about what to expect, and Dangchao
had chuckled at how effective the carnage was in
getting people to fall flat on their faces and lie
there until they were sure the guns had stopped,
the next time that the image "spoke".

"There will always be collateral damage in
military matters," he said, when people complained about innocent spectators being killed...
spectators who would have gladly bowed down if
they had only known what was expected of them.
"Isn't it interesting how quickly word is getting
around to other 'innocents'," he giggled, "now
that we have made examples of a few weaklings
who would hide behind their ignorance?"

The Antichrist had no qualms about killing a
few of his own faithful in order to make a point.
But what he desired most was to rid the world of
the terrible Twelve Tribes, who were gaining a
higher profile every day in their prophecies against
him. News of the amputations had reached him,
and he decreed that guillotines should be constructed in malls and shopping centres all over
the world. If believers were executed publicly,
and in great numbers, he reasoned, it would
successfully terrorise any of his followers who
might be considering defection.

Zion Ben-Jonah Writes

Powerful faith affects all with whom it comes in contact. Some will be inspired to imitate what they see; but most only become angry when they see such faith. They cannot live with the truth about their own spiritual poverty, and so they attack those who have shamed them. They call them heretics, fanatics, cults. And they seek to have them silenced, if not destroyed.

The Revelation talks of a great multitude which could not be numbered (in addition to the 144,000 saints who are sealed by God before the Great Tribulation begins). It says that these people will wear white robes when they stand before God, robes which have been washed clean in the "blood of the Lamb". (Revelation 7:9, 14-17)

The "blood of the Lamb" symbolises the blood that Jesus spilled for all of us when he was crucified. But Jesus also asked us to take up our own crosses and to follow in his footsteps. The Revelation says that during the Great Tribulation, believers will be able to spiritually triumph over the Antichrist "by the blood of the Lamb, and by the word of their testimony, and by the fact that they loved not their lives, even in the face of death." (Revelation 12:11)

All indications are that the great multitude that "comes out of great tribulation" will actually be martyrs, following the Lamb to their deaths. The Revelation specifically says of them that they will be "beheaded". (Revelation 20:4)

20. Disasters

Reinhard trudged wearily through the ankle-deep snow. All of Moscow was in a shambles. Hardly a building in the city had been spared.

First there were the meteorites, thousands of them scattered over all of Europe, North Africa, the Middle East, and some parts of Asia. They left craters wherever they hit, and caused forest fires over much of the planet. A cloud of haze had circled the earth, blocking out much of the sun's light. Warm air from the fires had forced precipitation far up into the atmosphere, where the moisture froze and refroze until it became huge hailstones weighing up to a kilogram apiece. Thousands died when the giant balls of ice finally rained down on the population. Whole cities were left without roofs. Cars by the millions were smashed beyond repair. Animals lay dead everywhere.

Then there was the big one, the asteroid itself. It landed in the mid-Atlantic, sending hundred metre high tidal waves across the ocean, completely swamping most coastal cities. Millions were lost on the east coast of South and Central America, and the west coast of Africa and Europe.

The second wave of meteorites or falling stars, was worse than the first, although they were all part of the same galactic storm that had been flying through space for aeons. In Russia, they were calling the disaster "Chernobyl" because of its radioactive composition. Radiation levels were dangerously high in a third of the earth's water supplies, and the problem was so widespread, that most people had little choice but to drink the contaminated water, even *knowing* that it would cause cancers, birth defects, and early deaths. It was often a choice between drinking it or dying of thirst.

Rayford and Chaim had predicted it all, and Dangchao and Pope Pius had done what they could to hush it up when they had learned that the asteroid really was on its way. Right up to the last, the experts were reported as saying that the chances of a direct hit were extremely small. They started with figures like one chance in a million, and the day before the first meteorites fell, they were still saying there was only one chance in ten that it would be a direct hit. By the time the seriousness of the situation had become clear, it was too late to evacuate most cities. And now Dangchao's brave new world was in total disarray.

It was because of his hatred for the Tribulation Force (whom Dangchao erroneously assumed were the original 144,000 tribal members) that this had happened in the first place.

At first Rayford and Chaim had declared a drought on Israel, that would continue until Dangchao ceased his plans to execute believers. Although the rain stopped and, as it happens, did not fall for three years, it did not stop preparations for the executions.

Then the Two promised that the drinking water would be cursed in the first city where an execution took place. The first executions took place in Amman, Jordan, with more than a hundred believers killed the first day. However, the same day, two monkeys were found dead in the town's water supply, after having escaped from a circus. Subsequent tests revealed that they had died from the ebola virus, and a deadly epidemic broke out which ended in all of Jordan being quarantined to contain it. Interestingly, executions in Jordan ceased, and there were no further executions of believers there throughout the final three years.

But Dangchao had bellowed out his anger against the believers even more after the Amman incident. Executions started in earnest all over the world over the next few days. In the space of a month, more than a million one-handed believers had been beheaded. Of course it was hardly a place of refuge, as deaths from the virus were as prevalent as were executions elsewhere.

And that was when the Two Witnesses decreed that the asteroid would hit. Dangchao and Pius, both of whom stubbornly refused to look at the Twelve Tribes website themselves, as though fearful that it would "brainwash" them, received regular reports on it from their advisers. When they had been informed about the asteroid prophecy, they put observatories on the alert around the world. Observatory personnel were told to keep information secret from the media and from other members of the public, but it did not work completely. The Press got the story five days before the asteroid hit. Nevertheless, it was still too late for the public to do much about it.

Now here was Reinhard, trudging through the snow in Moscow, on his way to a safe house, which had been damaged by the hailstones. It would be his job to organise repairs. Sheila Armitage was too old to undertake such tasks, and so the hard work was always left for him to do.

First it was Rayford, whom he had spent so much time teaching, only to have him take over the stage in directing the Jesans. Reinhard had done his best to accept it humbly at the time, but it wasn't much fun being left to get out the literature on the streets while Rayford went on teaching as though everything he said was his own ideas. Then it was Sheila. People just naturally turned to her for counsel in preference to himself, because she was almost twice as old as him. And lately it had been Jerry, one of the first recruits for the tribe of Asher, who was commanding more respect from tribal members than what Reinhard himself was getting.

Sure enough, when he arrived, Jerry, a strong, handsome man in his sixties, with long white hair and a beautiful white beard, already had everyone working hard at repairing and reconstructing the safe house. While neighbours pulled off damaged roofing, so they could replace it with plastic sheeting, or other materials purchased from government stores, Jerry's workers scoured the streets for the best of the discarded bits, to be used in repairing their own accommodation. Materials were already coming in, and it would not be long before the snow at least, would be kept out of their living quarters.

"Come in! Come in!" Jerry said kindly, when Reinhard gave the secret knock and Jerry had unlocked the door. "Ivan, get some coffee for our brother," the ex-American said in perfect Russian.

"I do not need coffee," Reinhard said abruptly. "I am here to vork."

"Certainly," Jerry said politely. Then he looked Reinhard in the eye: "Is something bothering you?"

"No, nothing is bothering me," Reinhard snapped. "Is something bothering *you*?"

"Well, yes, I guess it is," said Jerry. "Can we go into the back room to talk privately?"

"Vat's wrong vit talking right here vere ve are?" Reinhard asked as he sunk deeper into the soft chair, his hands extending the full length of both arms.

"I didn't want to embarrass you," Jerry replied, almost in a whisper. "I think you're upset about something, and I wanted to discuss it in private... just you and me."

Reinhard picked himself up and threw his body toward the back room. *I didn't want to embarrass you* he thought to himself. Typical of the smooth-talking Jerry Anthony. He just naturally assumed that he was right and that all of his lackey's would agree with him.

"Does it bother you that I'm leading here?" Jerry asked. He had been noticing the problem for several weeks, and it was time to address it.

"Maybe," Reinhard said, with a shrug of his shoulders, eyebrows, and lips, to indicate the insignificance he supposedly placed on the issue.

"Please, can I share something with you?" Jerry asked.

"Suit yourself," Reinhard replied, pretending to show no interest, as he leaned against a counter in the tiny workroom, and looked at the floor.

"Before the war... in America... I had what I thought was a good job. I saw myself as a good leader. But it took the war, and the deaths of a lot of innocent people to make me see that my ideas were all wrong. A fancy title does not make a person a leader.

"I came here, to Moscow, a lost and broken man. But when I met you, Reinhard," (and Jerry paused here for effect). "When I met you, I knew that I had found someone who was a *true* leader. You had no recognition as far as the world was concerned, no pay, no title, but you knew where you were going. You knew how to tell the important issues from the trivial ones, and you inspired me to try once more... to be a *true* leader.

Reinhard had been caught completely off guard. He had expected a rebuke from the older man. Instead, he had been flattered. It did more than any rebuke could have done to humble the young man. It had been a long time since Reinhard had received such a warm compliment, and he knew himself that what Jerry was saying about true leadership was right. Being a good leader did not depend on getting compliments or other positive recognition. It had more to do with catching sight of something that others were not aware of.

What Jerry had said was enough to bring back the vision to one who had let his flame go dim. Reinhard had seen others in the Twelve Tribes lose their vision of eternity, and heaven, and the return of Jesus, and they had each turned back. Some of them had been very good leaders before they had fallen away. He shuddered to think that he had been heading the same way himself. He reached out to hug the older man.

"Danke," he said, for Jerry knew German too. "Danke, Jerry! Please forgive me for my bad manner."

Reinhard had been very busy since he arrived in Moscow, more than four years earlier, but it was no excuse for his failure to have ever really shared deeply with this man who had been such a great help to the movement for more than three years, and who had just spoken the exact words that were needed to bring Reinhard out of his spiritual nosedive.

"Tell me about yourself," Reinhard said, in an effort to make up for the sins of his past. "How did you come to Moscow, of all places?"

"We did not have much choice," Jerry explained. I hid out in America for several weeks; but when a helicopter finally came to pick up survivors, it turned out to be a Russian one. We were brought here, and I have been here ever since."

"And vat about your family?" Reinhard asked?

"I had a daughter and a son, both living in New York City. They were near the centre of the blast. They would have died instantly."

"And your wife?"

"My wife?" Jerry asked blankly. "I... She..." And he hesitated. "I have never talked about it."

"Maybe dis vould be good time for starting," Reinhard suggested kindly.

Jerry hesitated once again. It was clear that he *wanted* to talk, but something was holding him back. "I do need to talk about it," he said. "Can you keep this just between you and me?" he asked. "It's very important."

"Certainly," Reinhard agreed.

"My wife was killed, not by the bomb. She was killed by an assassin, in front of my eyes." Jerry's voice was already beginning to break, but he wanted to finish his story. It obviously was something that he had kept inside for quite some time. "He meant to kill me too!" he sobbed. "Bob... one of my security men, threw himself in front of me."

Jerry sat on the floor and put his face in his hands, sobbing quietly as he spoke.

Reinhard listened in amazement. Security men? Assassins? What was he talking about?

"The explosion deafened me for a while. I was so traumatised that I could not speak. No one else got out of that bunker alive. When the Russians arrived, I knew I couldn't use my real name. So I used my middle name instead... Gerald Anthony.

My beard had already begun to grow, and so I kept it... along with the long hair.

Reinhard joined Jerry on the floor and reached out to hug him. Whatever the man was talking about, he was clearly deeply disturbed.

"How could God ever have forgiven me?" he wept, wiping his nose with a handkerchief.

"How could I have been so heartless? I let my own political ambitions become more important than the lives of all those people. I saw my error too late. I couldn't save America; but thank God, I didn't push the button to destroy *them*."

Reinhard was still trying to make sense of what Jerry was saying. How could Jerry Anthony or Jerry whoever he was think that he had caused the fall of America? He pushed the old man's hair back away from his face, and studied his features. His hair had gone completely grey, possibly from what he had been through, but under the beard Reinhard thought he could recognise him now.

"Fitzhugh?" he asked.

Jerry nodded.

Reinhard could hardly believe it. He was sitting on the workroom floor hugging the former President of the United States. The man was a bit older, and wore long hair and a beard now, but it *was* the President.

A suicide bomber (perhaps one of his own security men) must have entered the President's bunker under the White House, along with him and the First Lady.

The President of the United States had just told Reinhard that it was *Reinhard* who had taught him what it meant to be a leader. And he had said it after having worked quietly under Reinhard's leadership for more than three years. What an amazing compliment! And how foolish of him to have worried because he was not getting the recognition that he thought he had deserved!

Truly, what God had called him to do was more important than being the President of the most powerful country in the world... President Gerald Fitzhugh himself knew that. And what they were doing was important even if Reinhard was *not* the most widely recognised member of this new kingdom. Reinhard prayed for strength to stay faithful with even the humblest job, and he thanked God for the privilege of being able to serve in such an important movement.

*   *   *

In contrast, Dangchao and Pius were tortured men, spinning out of control in their obsession to *maintain* control of the world. Pius was almost as demonic as Dangchao now, having learned how to perform a few sensational tricks with the help of Dangchao's supernatural powers. Pius would unashamedly prostrate himself on the ground in front of the statue whenever walking through the Temple Complex now, and he had started bowing to Dangchao and using grandiose titles for him that became further evidence of his worship for this man/Beast.

The statue had survived the disasters, but both Temples had been damaged by the hail storm. A meteorite had destroyed Pius' personal residence when the first shower hit. Fortunately, he had not been there when it struck.

"We must stop them," Dangchao spluttered as he was eating lunch with his cohort. "We must find their headquarters... kill their *Two Witnesses*, as they call them. If we don't, they will continue to grow. Torture will do it. Someone must know. They'll tell us where it is."

"But, Your Worship," Pius replied, "torture takes time. It will slow down the executions. And everyone is needed for rebuilding. It takes a lot of infrastructure just to ferret them out to begin with. There are interviews with informers, office staff to maintain records, arresting officers, executioners. Even the morgues are overcrowded with these latest disasters."

"Damn the disasters! Let them lie where they are! If we don't stop these Christians, everything else will be wasted. Skip the red tape too. If an informer even *thinks* that someone is connected with the movement, I want that person killed. I don't care whether they have a Mark or not. There must be people on the inside helping them. We must find them and make examples of them."

Dangchao continued: "The people can rebuild later. All of *our* energies must be put into stopping these Christians. If we don't do that, there won't be a world *left* to rebuild."

And so, while the world looked on in shocked disbelief, their great leader --the man they had all thought as recently as a year and a half ago was the greatest leader the world had ever known -- chose to ignore their suffering because of his own obsession with getting back at the Christians.

Dangchao had convinced himself that it was the Christians who were destroying the world, and he used his best speech writers and press secretaries to get that message across to the masses. He succeeded in whipping up such hysterical hatred for Christians and such paranoia about their supposed conspiracy against the rest of the world, that soon neighbours were turning one another in for execution on the flimsiest of evidence. Executions increased tenfold, but eight out of ten of the people being killed now were ones who bore the mark in their very much *intact* right hands!

The effect of Dangchao's rage was to encourage even more of his faithful followers to defect. If they were going to die anyway, they reasoned, it would be better to die on the side of right.

And the Two Witnesses could not resist echoing the timeless wisdom of such reasoning. "If we are all going to die anyway," they said, "then how much better to die for God than to die for a demon? This has been the common sense behind the gospel message for centuries, whether or not the world happens to be falling apart around us."

Zion Ben-Jonah Writes

The disasters that are heralded by the first four "trumpets" of the Great Tribulation (Revelation 8:6-12) are mentioned in this chapter. It is interesting that the word "chernobyl" is the Russian name for the poisonous "wormwood" plant. The passage from Revelation 8 says that the asteroid that hits the earth will be called Wormwood.

This chapter also reveals a little more of the powers that the Two Witnesses will be able to wield. Read about them in Revelation 11:6.

The main lesson, however, is that of leadership. The beastly systems of the world all jostle for power, wealth, fame, and honour. But the humble, sacrificial death of the "Lamb" is what characterises the kingdom of heaven.

What a shame that Constantine did not have the opportunity to learn as Fitzhugh does in this chapter, what it means to be a true leader in the kingdom of heaven! Only when that happens will people understand that it would be better for the leaders of the most powerful countries and empires in history to be humble missionaries and servants in the kingdom of heaven than to supposedly "use their power" to bring favours for God and for his people.

Pius represents the tragic end that befalls those who refuse to leave their positions of power along with everything else that God calls us to forsake in order to enter his kingdom.

21. Apollyon

The battle between Dangchao and the Christians was on in earnest, and it continued that way as the countdown toward the end of the three and a half years of Tribulation continued.

In the two years from the time that Dangchao had first caused the sacrifices to cease, and had moved into the Temple in Jerusalem, both sides had lost count of the millions who had chosen to reject the Mark, and the millions more who had been executed to appease Dangchao's rage.

Although Pius was slightly more sane than the Antichrist himself, he was also becoming addicted to the sickening pleasure that came with conducting such a worldwide Inquisition. It was the thrill of pure, unadulterated power that attracted them now, except that in their case, it was very much impure and very much adulterated *use* of power that had made it all so evil.

But, although Dangchao and Pius were killing many more people than Rayford and Chaim were converting, the Christians were clearly winning the spiritual battle. The numbers of people asking to become a part of the Tribulation Force were growing every day in *spite* of the killings.

The asteroid and meteorite showers had left millions dead and widespread destruction. Neither the U.N. nor the governments of its individual member nations seemed capable of dealing with the problems that flowed on from the disasters. The world appeared to be heading back to the Dark Ages. People everywhere were disillusioned. Dangchao was definitely slipping in the popularity stakes.

But dissatisfaction with the new world order was not the main reason why people were choosing to become followers of Jesus. People joining the Tribulation Force were primarily moved by the testimony of those who went before them... a testimony that shone forth even at their executions. Surely there *was* something beyond this life, and these followers of Jesus had found it!

The Two Witnesses, far from being spooked by Dangchao and Pius' show of strength and by their cruel efforts to locate them, had actually announced simultaneous press conferences, one in Sydney and one in London.

The frenzied response from the media showed how little control Dangchao had over the Press as well. Troops were sent to break up both conferences and to arrest or kill Rayford and Chaim; but in both cases, it was the troops who were destroyed, as the Two Witnesses simply spoke a word and soldiers fell to the ground, their insides eaten out by maggots.

When it came time for Chaim and Rayford to leave their respective press conferences, they spoke once more and everyone present became temporarily blind. In the ensuing confusion, the Two Witnesses merely walked away, unnoticed.

The press conferences themselves were an overwhelming success for the Christian cause.

The Two Witnesses exuded such an air of calm and confidence throughout their respective interviews that the whole world could not help but be impressed. What they said, from opposite ends of the world, was almost the same. They explained in clear simple language that all God wanted was for people to give him the honour that he deserved as their Creator. They said that Dangchao and Pius and others like them were only God's *puppets*, placed on earth to test the faith of each individual. And they finished with a heartfelt plea for people to turn from their service to the Antichrist and his Mark and to put their faith totally in God and in his Son, Jesus, before the next curse fell on each of them personally. They did not specify what form the curse would take.

"You will be wishing that you could die to escape it," Rayford promised. "I would not want to wish it on anyone. But it is going to happen. Believe me. You have a very short time to repent. Please, for your own good, turn now. Even cutting your hand off would be nothing by comparison to what awaits you if you don't turn now."

The press conference, which included live broadcasts all over the world, resulted in the biggest influx into the Tribulation Force that the Christians had so far experienced. There were too many for the Twelve Tribes to handle on their own; so, some of the people who had already undergone amputations themselves were being called in to assist with operations.

It did not take long for the rest of the world to become aware of the increased support for the Christian cause.

Dangchao, who had been fuming ever since the press conferences, was out of his mind.

"*Puppets*, are we?" he shouted, a few weeks after Rayford and Chaim were first reported to have called him that. He threw yet another newspaper down after reading the hated word.

"Puppets? How dare they!" He threw his hands into the air and his head back in frustration as he shouted. The media had taken up that one word and woven it into just about every report that came out about the Twelve Tribes after that.

Dangchao went on a rampage through his palatial drawing room, kicking furniture and knocking things over. He smashed a heavy vase into a large mirror. Pius looked on almost indifferently now. He was growing accustomed to Dangchao's rages, and he had even had a few himself.

"I'll show them who the puppets are, and who pulls the strings! I'll show them!" Dangchao shouted.

"Apollyon! Get up here! *Apollyon!*"

"Yes, Master!" And suddenly at Dangchao's right hand stood a creature that could only be a fierce and powerful demon. Its face was uglier than anything that Pius had ever seen before... apart from Dangchao's other face. Pius shrunk back into a dark corner, hoping that the creature would not take notice of him.

"Apollyon, bring up your troops!"

"You mean bring them up *here*?" Apollyon asked in disbelief.

"Yes, bring them up here!" Dangchao shouted. And his face assumed the grotesque form that Pius so feared. "I want the world to know how much power I have. I want them to taste what I can do to them. And I want to teach those Christians a lesson."

"But they'll hurt *our* people too, Master," Apollyon said. "Do we really want to do that now? Before time?"

"I know what I'm doing!" Dangchao shouted. "If I can't send them to hell, I can at least bring hell to them!" He was overcome with amusement at his own turn of phrase, breaking into one of his fits of demonic laughter. "They're taking people away from me. But I can have the satisfaction of tormenting them now... *before* they die!" And the laughter resumed once more.

Pius was not so sure about the wisdom of tormenting their own people; but if Dangchao's plan would bring some suffering to the *aliens*... (Pius' name for the Two Witnesses; he never used the term Christian when referring to the believers, because it reminded him of what he had once claimed to be.) If Dangchao's plan would bring suffering to the Twelve Tribes, then it was worth a lot of "collateral damage", as Dangchao liked to call it.

"*Now*, Apollyon! Do it *now!*" Dangchao bellowed, and his demon face lit up as he prepared to watch what followed.

The floor of the room split down the middle, tearing the carpet and splintering the floorboards. Smoke came out... dense, black smoke; and it filled the room, filled the palace, poured out into the street; and eventually filled nearly all of Jerusalem. People could barely breathe.

And then, out of the smoke there came the sound of troops, a kind of rhythmic beating of hooves, and the metallic bumping and scraping of armour. It sounded distant and faint at first, but then it grew in intensity. People at the limits of the smoke were the first to see what the sound was coming from, and they instinctively turned to run.

It was a great cloud of locusts... or at least creatures that resembled locusts. But they were a strange mutation. Their armoured bodies and metallic wings made them sound like knights on horseback when they flew in a horde as they were at the moment. On their tails were stingers like those on a scorpion.

These locusts did not attack crops or grass or trees. Instead, they attacked people. They had tiny sharp teeth that they used to get a hold on someone before jabbing their poisonous stinger in. The pain was unbearable... worse even than the pain of childbirth. The poison paralysed their limbs as well, making it impossible for victims to do more than roll on the ground in agony for the two or three hours it took for the pain to wear off. Pain-killers were largely ineffectual, and there was no known antidote.

Many would be stung over and over, despite every attempt to escape the horrible plague.

The locusts kept coming out of the thick, black cloud all that day. They left Jerusalem in separate hordes, each one going in a different direction. They would each work their way around the world over the next five months, stinging all who were in their way.

All, that is, except the members of the Twelve Tribes. Perhaps it was some residue from the tiny transponder that these creatures were attracted to. Or perhaps it was divine protection for the 144,000. In either case, it did not take long before Rayford, Chaim, and the media had recognised the irony of the trap that Dangchao had fallen into.

Rayford and Chaim had predicted great suffering over all of the earth... suffering that would be so painful that people would wish they could die. *They* had pronounced the curse, but Dangchao himself had been the "puppet" through which it had become reality! His own tiny alien creatures with their metal wings, sharp teeth, and scorpion tails were the instrument through which God gave the world a taste of what hell would be like. At the same time, God had protected the people who were the target of Dangchao's hate!

The Tribulation Force were not, as were the Twelve Tribes, totally immune to the locusts, but the pain for them seemed to be little more than a bee sting by comparison to what others felt.

When Christians, whether from the Twelve Tribes or from the Tribulation Force, came upon others who had been stung, they offered comfort, prayer, and whatever practical assistance they could give. It did not take away the pain, but it became a powerful testimony, not only of God's power to protect his own, but also of the love that the Christians had, even for their enemies.

The rest of the world... those who had not converted to faith in Jesus by this time... were, indeed, becoming more and more evil.... more and more "enemies" of God and of all who would follow Him. Every kindness from the Christians only increased their hatred.

Although countless millions had converted to faith in Jesus by this time, the majority of the earth's population continued to support Dangchao and his policies. They believed his lies about the Two Witnesses being the cause of all of the earth's problems, and they felt and expressed nothing but hatred for God.

The three and a half years of the Great Tribulation were only a year away from completion by the time the locust plague had ceased. Five months after they had arrived, the locusts returned to Jerusalem, each having circled the globe. It was like a rewind of their arrival. Another cloud of thick, black smoke covered the city; they flew into it; and then the cloud of smoke disappeared down through the hole in Dangchao's palace, taking the fearsome creatures with it.

Zion Ben-Jonah Writes

The description of the "locusts" is quite detailed in The Revelation (9:7-10). They may be mutant insects, demons (i.e. fallen angels) or even tormented souls trapped inside tiny little machines, as the description of them each having human faces suggests.

For a world that has largely assumed that hell is a fairy tale and that the devil is a joke, this chapter may be a bit hard to swallow... possibly even infuriating.

But consider what it would have sounded like two hundred years ago, if we had talked of cell phones and computer graphics, jets, atomic bombs, and laser images. God's technology is light years ahead of our own, and so there may yet be some big surprises for those of us living in the confines of what little Twenty-First Century science can tell us about life, the universe, and everything.

We personally believe that God acts in accord with his own rules. But we also believe that only God has the complete rule book. And so there may be dimensions that we have not even begun to fathom yet.

Witches, fairies, UFO sightings, and other psychic phenomena are being taken quite seriously by many these days. So why rule out the possibility of angels, devils, curses and divine protection, especially when they come from a source that is as otherwise reliable as is the Bible?

22. Journey to Jerusalem

For nearly three and a half years now, death and destruction had become a way of life throughout the entire world. More lives had been lost in violent deaths during that period than in all the wars throughout history.

In England, towns like Swansea and Plymouth had been virtually washed off the map by the big wave. Cities like Liverpool had also suffered great damage and loss of life. England had done a better job of rebuilding than other countries (mostly in Africa and South and Central America) which had also been severely damaged by the wave; but that did not say much in itself. Disposing of all the bloated bodies had become the first priority. Reconstruction was largely put on hold.

Deserted coastal towns were popular haunts for the Tribulation Force, who found shelter and escape from public exposure by squatting in them. They were able to fish for sustenance, even if they could not find discarded food as easily as they could in the big cities.

The United Nations had declared England to be an "international country" shortly after the fall of America, which effectively meant that it was under strict U.N. control. U.N. troops enforced conformity with all of its official policies. And U.N. policies were always determined by General Secretary Levi Xu Dangchao.

England had lost a further ten million people to the U.N. executions.

All of this had the effect of numbing people to the full impact of death. For those who chose to follow Dangchao, it meant that they had hardened their hearts even to the cries of children and babies being cruelly and callously murdered. When their own loved ones were lost, they only became more angry with God.

Numbness for the Christians meant that they lived with a constant appreciation of eternal values -- something they had not given much thought to in the days when life had been easier. Death, especially such a quick one as performed by the guillotine, was an express ticket to heaven. There was no future for them on earth, apart from getting others to join in their dramatic statement of faith in God and rejection of all that Dangchao's regime stood for.

But it was still as though everyone -- good and bad alike -- was living in a constant state of shock.

The saddest thing about the executions were the children. Parents would often have to hold their own babies in the neck groove at the bottom of the death machine, because the gap was too big for their tiny heads. The children, of course, had not yet received the mark. But the rules were that all orphans of the Tribulation Force were to be forcibly given the mark and then raised in government orphanages.

The authorities really did not want the responsibility for so many babies and children, but they took an evil delight in forcing parents to make the choice themselves about whether to sacrifice their children to the authorities or to the guillotine. Most chose the guillotine.

Older children (those over seven) were allowed to make their own choice. Most chose to go with the authorities, and that caused more anguish for the Tribulation Force than did the guillotine.

The saints came to see the significance of a warning that Jesus had given, instructing believers to pray that they would not be pregnant or have small children in the period just before the Great Tribulation.

Sexual activity did not cease altogether amongst the believers, but it did become much rarer than it had been before the troubles started. No one wanted to have a child in such awful times, and birth control was a luxury that few of the saints could afford. The crowded living conditions did not leave much opportunity for privacy either.

Those facing execution had far more serious thoughts on their minds. And the *Twelve Tribes* had earlier adopted a policy of discouraging marriage, and banning romantic dalliances. If a couple wished to pursue a relationship, they were assigned to work duties together, always with chaperones present or nearby. If a decision was made to marry, it was made without any kissing or cuddling. A simple ceremony would be performed as soon as possible after a decision was made.

Married couples in the Twelve Tribes were expected to put the cause above their relationship. They were often separated for long periods of time; but they only needed to remind themselves of how hard life was for the Tribulation Force to get things back into perspective.

There were a few tribal members who fell away. But that only strengthened the resolve of those who remained.

And there were physical casualties amongst the Twelve Tribes too. Although not a single person who had refused the Mark had been stung by the locusts, there *were* tribal members who had been caught during police raids, when they were visiting or assisting the Tribulation Force, and there were one or two incidents where security had been breached and a whole base had been taken into custody. Death, in such circumstances, was inevitable; but authorities were more inclined to torture those who did not have the Mark, believing that they had more information on where the leaders were located.

Some had given in under torture, resulting in more arrests; but such defections were rare.

New converts at the start of the final three and a half years (ones who had not taken the Mark) were enough to fill in for any losses in the Twelve Tribes' numbers, so that, with a year to go, they still numbered close to 144,000.

But during that last year, their numbers dropped dramatically. They were all that remained of the holdouts... the only people on earth who had refused the Mark. And even *they* were rapidly dying out.

"What happened to our protection?" Chloe asked in an urgent email to Rayford when Mary Teresa was shot and killed in a raid in Rome.

"Protection is not absolute," Rayford had written to all of the tribes in response. "God still lets his rain fall on the just and on the unjust. Any army that has ever won a war has still had its casualties, and we have had them too. But look how far we have come. God is surely with us.

"The word 'survivor' literally means 'one who lives above'. We can physically stay alive, and that would be a form of survival. But there is an even greater triumph that comes from facing the final enemy -- death -- and still coming out on top. The message of the resurrection is that death is *not* the end. It makes all the difference.

"As the Apostle Paul has said, if there is no resurrection, then we are, of all people, most miserable. But because there *is* a resurrection, we will live on -- even after they have taken our lives. We will survive! We will live *above* it all!"

Nevertheless, every surviving member of the Twelve Tribes was counting down the days over those final months.

When there were just two weeks to go, Rayford and Chaim felt it was time to head for Jerusalem.

They both knew that it would end in their deaths, and so, when they bid farewell to their respective co-workers, it was with heavy hearts. Irene was surprisingly peaceful about Rayford's departure. In fact, she was the one who reminded *him* that they had had much more time together than most of the other couples they knew. "Count the days," she said as he pulled away from their final embrace. "Count the days."

The Two Witnesses left behind their computers -- their only communication link with the rest of the Twelve Tribes. They took a change of clothes and a few toiletries -- nothing more. Rayford was able to hitch-hike the entire way; but Chaim needed to board a plane to get out of Australia.

Chaim had never been married, and possibly because of that, he had a closer relationship with his co-workers. His tears flowed freely when he said goodbye to his co-workers. He was older than Rayford, with long brown hair and a beard, that had grown of necessity when they ran out of razor blades. "It just seemed natural to let my hair grow too," he said.

Chaim walked into Kingsford Smith Airport in Sydney, on a warm Sunday afternoon in late November. He was not sure how he was going to get out of the country. He had no ticket, no passport, no visa, no money, not even any identification, and most important, no Mark. He got as far as the departure lounges without incident.

Australian Immigration had ceased checking documents for departing passengers a few years earlier.

He located a flight with El Al going to Tel Aviv via Bangkok. When passengers were called to board, Chaim took his place in the queue. A woman in front of him had a seizure of some sort just as her ticket was being checked. While airline staff occupied themselves with her, Rayford slipped past the check-in desk and into the hallway that led to the plane. It was as easy as that. The flight was not heavily booked, so Chaim waited in the plane's rest room till all other passengers were seated, and then he took an unoccupied seat next to the aisle.

The plane took off for Bangkok without incident. It reached its desired altitude, and then levelled out. Rayford was thanking God for how smoothly it had all gone when a stewardess came and leaned over his seat. "We have no record of a passenger in this seat," she said quietly. "Have you moved from some other seat?"

"No, this is the only seat I've been in," Chaim responded, smiling up at the woman with a mischievous twinkle in his eye.

"Can I see your boarding pass?" the stewardess asked.

"I'm afraid I don't have one," Chaim replied, still smiling.

The stewardess looked concerned. "Can you show me your ticket?"

"Truth is, I don't have a ticket either," Chaim answered sweetly.

"Please wait here," the stewardess said as she hurried off to get a second opinion before proceeding further.

I wonder where she thinks I would go up here, Chaim thought to himself as he waited.

In the galley, Hattie, the stewardess, pulled David, the chief steward out to where he could look down the aisle toward the rear of the plane.

"See that man in the middle aisle seat about six rows back?" Hattie whispered. "He doesn't have a ticket."

"Really?" said the steward, as if that explained everything. "See, I noticed him when he got on. Thought at the time that he looked like one of those Witness blokes. Didya see them on T.V.?"

"Oh yeah!" said Hattie, as she studied Chaim's features. Chaim noticed the two staring at him and he fluttered his fingers in a friendly wave.

"This should be interesting," David whispered as he walked back toward where Chaim was sitting.

"You're one of the Witnesses, aren't you?" David asked. "I've visited your website."

He glanced at Hattie, who encouraged him by saying, "No big deal, David. Everybody has."

"Thank you," said Chaim, who shook David's extended hand.

"So what are you doing on this plane?" David asked.

"Flying to Tel Aviv. I have some business in Jerusalem."

"But you really do need a ticket to fly."

"You must know that I can't buy a ticket without the Mark; and I don't have the Mark."

"I'll have to report this to my superiors, and they'll probably want us to turn around and take you back to Sydney. Even if they agree to let you stay on, they'll have police waiting for you in Bangkok. You do realise that, don't you?"

"Don't you think God can get me to Jerusalem?" Chaim asked as he looked up at David with his head tilted to one side?

"Well, I've heard stories... and I sure wouldn't want to get you angry!" he laughed. "But certainly you wouldn't do something dangerous here, not on the plane, would you?"

"To tell you the truth," Chaim said, as he indicated for David to bend closer so he could hear a whisper, "I really don't have much control over it. I only know moments before it happens. I figure that only God knows just how much protection I need."

"Look, what I'll do is have a talk with the Captain and then get back to you," the younger man replied.

"Thank you," Chaim smiled, and then he went back to reading the newspaper that he had been reading during take-off.

In the cockpit there was a hurried exchange of information and then a call to Sydney.

"He says that there could be a show of force," said the Captain.

Instructions came through that they should do nothing to upset Chaim, and that they should proceed on to Bangkok, where authorities would be notified.

However, a zealous airline employee in Sydney phoned Israel too, and suggested that word be sent through to the palace. By the time the plane touched down in Bangkok at 10pm local time, instructions had been changed. Chaim was to be kept on the plane for the midnight flight to Tel Aviv. A welcoming party was being arranged by the authorities at Ben Gurion Airport the following morning.

Meanwhile, someone in Tel Aviv had leaked the story to the media, and word on TV was that Chaim had *hijacked* the plane. Half the reporters in Israel were at the airport, along with what looked like half of the U.N.'s sizeable military presence.

When the plane finally touched down at Tel Aviv, it taxied to a domestic lounge which had been sealed off overnight. Chaim was then allowed to exit on his own, before the plane proceeded to the international terminal with the other passengers.

Chaim came through the door into the arrival lounge and blinked at the flashing cameras and bright television lights. He waved to the press, and then a U.N. official came forward, trying to look strong for the sake of the cameras, and yet trying to look non-threatening for fear of Chaim's special powers.

"I'm afraid that you are going to have to come with me," he said, as he braced for a reaction.

"Certainly," Chaim responded. He was handcuffed and led to a police paddy wagon.

He was then taken, not to the police station, but to the palace itself, in Jerusalem.

"So! At last we meet!" gloated Dangchao as Chaim was led into his throne room. Everyone else bowed on the floor before the General Secretary, while Chaim remained standing.

"Where is your partner?" Dangchao asked.

"I don't know," Chaim answered honestly.

"Maybe I should hold you here for a few days, and see if he turns up."

Chaim did not respond.

"We could have some fun with you at the Temple," he said with an evil glint in his eye.

"And God could have some fun with you," Chaim replied, with a confidence that matched that of his captor. Dangchao caught the seriousness of the threat and eased back.

"Only kidding," he said. "I just want to ask your friend some questions. We really need to work *together*... for the good of the whole world."

Again Chaim remained silent.

News reports stated that Chaim had been arrested and that he was being detained at the palace. Dangchao was hopeful that it would be enough to attract Rayford.

Zion Ben-Jonah Writes

Of the Great Tribulation, Jesus promised that Christians would be betrayed and killed for their faith (Luke 21:16), and then he says (in verse 18), "but there shall not a hair of your head perish." The apparent contradiction is explained when we understand, as Rayford is quoted as saying in this chapter, that "protection is not absolute".

We may die for our faith, but we will not "perish". That is the essence of "living above". There is no air-tight guarantee that we will not suffer. In fact, indications are just the opposite (II Timothy 3:12). Ultimately, our protection will be spiritual and eternal, and not necessarily temporal.

This is why a "tribulation" vision is so important for all believers, in every age. When we stop trying to escape discomfort, and start to face even death itself, we will sort ourselves out spiritually. Life for most of us today has to do with more and more comforts, more and more luxuries, and less and less preparation for death.

The Bible says of the world in Noah's day and in the days of Sodom and Gomorrah that they were just too busy getting married and raising families to think of the things of God; and it was because of that (and not specifically homosexuality or atheism) that God destroyed them. (Luke 17:26-30)

Even the Two Witnesses will have their limitations, as Chaim experiences in this chapter.

23. The Rapture

It was Thursday morning before Rayford reached Jerusalem. He had taken that long to hitch-hike through Europe and the Middle East. Having heard on the way about Chaim's capture, Rayford headed straight for the palace when he arrived in the holy city.

On his journey through Europe, only two people had recognised him, and they had not presented a problem. But Rayford wasn't in Jerusalem half an hour before people started to point at him and whisper. As he walked, a crowd followed, to see what would happen. Someone phoned the media, and word was relayed to the palace, which seemed to be where Rayford was heading.

Strangely, no one dared touch, speak to, or even come close to Rayford as he walked. There was something about his gait that made those in his way immediately stand back to give him room.

When he arrived at the wide steps leading up to the palace entrance, he was faced with a huge media and military welcome. Cameras clicked and whirred as Dangchao appeared at the top of the steps, flanked by more than a dozen armed guards. Other U.N. snipers were perched at every available lookout point.

"Welcome! Welcome!" shouted Dangchao magnanimously, for the benefit of the public.

"I have come for Chaim Rosenberg!" shouted Rayford. "Bring him out here!"

"He's inside. Please come in!" Dangchao said as he walked down the steps to get closer to Rayford.

Rayford sat down on the pavement at the bottom of the steps. As his seat touched the ground a rumble suddenly shook the whole area. Everyone who was standing in the vicinity fell over, with the exception of Dangchao, who barely managed to regain his balance. Snipers fell from perches around the palace entrance, some of them seriously injured. Others picked up their weapons and scrambled quickly back to their feet.

"Bring Chaim here," Rayford said again, pointing to the ground beside where he sat. "*Now!*"

And another tremor sent those who had resumed standing back to the ground. This time Dangchao fell too. Some cameras being held by reporters who were wise enough to have stayed on the ground, caught pictures of the General Secretary falling spread-eagled in front of the Witness for the West. Rayford sat regally, with his legs folded in front of him.

"All right! All right." said Dangchao, as he struggled to a more dignified lotus position, facing Rayford.

"Bring the prisoner!" he said to one of his guards, and the man hurried up the steps.

"Don't worry. You'll get your chance," Rayford said. "Very soon. But for now, you are only going to bring more troubles on yourself if you don't turn Chaim over to me."

"Shoot him!" Dangchao shouted, as loudly as he could. But at the same instant, Rayford merely breathed out and a supersonic jet of flame shot straight toward Dangchao. The Antichrist ducked at lightning speed, and missed the flame, but it split just as quickly into several different directions. Then, moving more quickly than any human could react, the various tongues of flame sought out each of the soldiers who had a gun aimed at Rayford. They were all engulfed in flames before they had a chance to pull a trigger.

"You really shouldn't make me do that," Rayford said calmly to Dangchao.

"What are your plans?" Dangchao asked, obviously shaken. "If you will promise not to leave the city, I'll let your friend go with you."

"You'll let my friend come with me *regardless*," Rayford answered quietly. "But if it'll make you feel any better, we don't have any plans to leave the city for the next ten days."

Just then, Chaim appeared with the guard at the top of the steps.

Dangchao had no choice but to submit to the demands of the Two Witnesses; but later that day, his spin doctors made it sound like the two men were just free on bail pending a trial. There was outrage from some that a dangerous hijacker and suspected killer should be allowed to roam free; but Dangchao insisted that everything was under control. Of course it *was*... except that he wasn't the one holding the controls.

For the next six days Chaim and Rayford spent most of their time in the area around the Temple Mount, where they were able to address large crowds of people. It was early December, and the weather was cold; but the Two Witnesses stayed out on the streets, sleeping in shifts. They had accumulated a few rags, bits of firewood, and other materials to insulate themselves against the cold. They kept a little campfire going over-night, on the pavement where they slept. Which-ever one was not sleeping would stay awake to mind the fire; and to address the crowds.

Throughout the night people gathered to gawk at them and to listen, out of curiosity, to their pronouncements against the Dangchao govern-ment and against those who had put their faith in it. Twice someone had tried to attack them, and twice the attacker had been destroyed by fire. Word spread quickly through the media, and even more quickly amongst the spectators; so that the crowds barely dared to ask questions of the two prophets after that... until late on the following Wednesday night.

Rayford and Chaim had not been in email contact with the rest of the saints since they had left for Jerusalem ten days earlier. They ate little and prayed constantly over those final days. The Christians all knew that the time for Chaim and Rayford's demise was very near. There had been more deaths and defections amongst their own members over the past ten days too.

Irene and Elaine had both been taken by the authorities and executed a week after Rayford had left London. A few saints in Jerusalem had been able to sneak messages to the two men during that final week. News of Irene's death had added to the strain upon Rayford; but he did not stop preaching.

Matthew had been left more or less in charge of the Twelve Tribes *and* the Tribulation Force after Irene and Elaine disappeared; but the general feeling was that everything was falling apart. There were still four days to go before the long-awaited return of Jesus... *if* their calculations were correct, and some were wondering if they would last even that long without their beloved leaders.

Then, on Wednesday evening of that final week, one of two U.N. guards who were part of a round-the-clock watch over the Two Witnesses, drew a bead on Rayford with his rifle, just for fun. He was in a position where he could not be seen by Rayford himself, and Chaim was sleeping beside the fire. Just then, his companion bumped him, and the gun went off, shooting Rayford through the head. Rayford fell to the ground with a quiet thud.

"You've killed him!" whispered the other guard. "Look, you've killed him!" And then he saw Chaim begin to stir. "Quick! Get the other one before he gets up and burns you!"

"It's him or me, isn't it?" the soldier said as he pulled the trigger a second time. And Chaim too slumped over next to Rayford. He had also been shot in the head.

Rayford had just finished giving a speech to a small crowd before the shooting occurred, and the audience had been moving away at the precise moment when the shot rang out. Those few people who were still present to see Rayford, and then Chaim, fall could not believe their eyes. After three and a half years of fruitless tracking by the authorities, and after equally fruitless attempts to destroy these two men, one foolhardy soldier had eliminated them both, half by accident, in a matter of seconds with just two bullets!

The two soldiers rushed to establish that they really had killed the Two Witnesses, and then they notified their superiors. A military ambulance arrived and took the bodies and the two soldiers away, and a report went out to the media that the world had been saved; the Two Aliens (as Pius liked to call them) were dead.

Dangchao was up all night, addressing the media and making other arrangements. Early the next morning he unveiled a hastily constructed cyclone fence which surrounded the bodies of the Two Witnesses. They had been returned to where they had died. The embers of a campfire were still there; and the paraphernalia that the men had collected to keep themselves warm were scattered around inside the enclosure. The public was invited to view the scene for themselves. Soldiers who had been rostered to watch the two men were now being used to control the crowd flow.

Dangchao had decided to display the bodies because he feared that the Christians would try to start another resurrection story, as they had done with their Jesus. He also wanted people to know that it really was the Two Witnesses who had been killed, and that they really were dead.

But he went one step further. Christmas was only a few weeks away, and although it had been renamed Winterfest years earlier, he felt that this was a good time to change the *date* for the celebrations. He announced that the next day, Friday, would henceforth become the new date for celebrating Winterfest. Stores would remain open all day on this particular Friday, for last minute shopping; but all non-essential businesses would be closed for Thursday and Friday both. This gave people two days in which to buy their gifts, food, and drinks, to celebrate the holiday. Everyone loved it. The stores experienced the greatest two-day shopping spree the world had ever known.

People were convinced that the human race had turned the corner. Peace and prosperity were going to return! And so they shopped with reckless abandon as they celebrated mankind's final victory over the "Aliens".

Festivities began that same day, and they grew more wild over the next two days. By Saturday afternoon, when the shops had all closed and even store staff were free to join in the celebrations, the whole world was in one big drunken, drug-crazed orgy.

But on Sunday morning, something startling happened in the Middle East. Over a stretch of fifteen hundred miles in all directions (reaching as far as Baghdad, Cairo, and Ankara), when people looked up, all they could see was what looked like a glass ceiling miles above the earth, stretching from horizon to horizon. Some light filtered through the glass, making it possible to see that there were structures and some movement on the other side.

Aeroplanes flying at altitudes above 25,000 feet had been forced to descend steeply or to turn back when they neared the Middle East.

Dangchao had a hurried meeting with his best military advisers, who were convinced the structure was an alien star ship the size of a small planet. The big question was whether or not the aliens manning it were friendly. Dangchao sensed what was up straightaway, and he encouraged the military to prepare for the worst.

Then, shortly after noon, there was a new development at the Temple Mount. Someone reported seeing movement in the hand of one of the Two Witnesses. Dangchao was alerted and he hurried to the site, along with an entourage of advisers and Press representatives.

Everyone gathered around and watched for a full five minutes without any sign of movement. They were about to chalk the report up to someone's over-active imagination when a barely perceptible tremor shook Chaim's body.

"Did you see that?" someone shouted. Indeed, Dangchao had seen it, and he was worried.

"Shoot him!" he shouted, pointing at Chaim.

"But he's already dead!" his guard argued. He, too, was scared. He had heard what happened to others who had tried to kill the Two Witnesses.

"I don't care if he's dead or not. Shoot him!" Dangchao shouted once again. He grabbed the gun out of the guard's hand, in an effort to do the job himself. He pointed it straight at Chaim's head and squeezed the trigger. But just as he did, the earth dropped out from under him. He threw his hands (and the gun) into the air to catch his balance. The ground began to shake, and the two bodies on the ground shook with it.

An earthquake! thought Dangchao. That's all it was. The bodies had *not* moved! It was only the earth shaking them.

But a moment later both Chaim's and Rayford's arms and legs started to move simultaneously. Their bodies straightened out, and their arms moved in unison to lift themselves up... up onto their knees. They were still kneeling, but otherwise erect as they opened their eyes and looked straight into the face of the Antichrist.

The single bullet-wound to each of their heads disappeared before Dangchao's eyes. Their hair became thicker, as grey streaks disappeared. Wrinkles vanished, and they both appeared to be no more than thirty years old. The ragged clothes they were wearing fell away to reveal a shimmering white robe.

The men rose to their full stature, as a voice boomed out of nowhere and everywhere at the same time: "Come up here!" Everyone instinctively looked up, and from the bottom of the glass ceiling, directly over the Temple Mount a big round opening appeared. It looked like a jet of white smoke shooting down from the opening toward the ground. But as the "smoke" got closer, it separated into millions of tiny beings, all dressed in white. In the middle of them was One whose appearance was almost blinding, as light radiated from Him. The other beings circled around him as he dropped lower and lower.

Chaim and Rayford began to rise up to meet the beings in the air. As they rose, they could see others like themselves ascending from the earth and then converging toward the Being of Light.

Most of the others were dressed in the shimmering white of the resurrected. But there were a few who were distinguishable by their everyday dress. These were the living saints. They, too, had undergone a transformation as they returned to the strength and beauty of their youth. Deformities and blemishes disappeared. Everyone taking part in this amazing gathering in the air experienced an overwhelming sensation of health and fitness. And, the best news for many was that there were *no missing limbs.*

Down on the ground, the earth was continuing to shake, much more violently now. The entire city of Jerusalem was trembling like the toy that it was in comparison to a city that was infinitely more power-ful floating in the air above it. Buildings began to collapse. From above, where the saints were, it looked like a tenth of the city was falling in slow motion. But down on the ground there was a deadly shower of glass, concrete, bricks and steel girders from the city's crumbling structures, raining down on the local population. People still recovering from the celebrations of the weekend were trapped or crushed in buildings all over Jerusalem.

The saints were too far above the earth to survive without external warmth and oxygen masks now. But there was no sensation that even approached freezing, nor were they struggling for breath.

All of the supernatural bodies were converging toward the Being of Light. Rayford, Chaim and the multitudes gathering around them all knew who it was. It was their Saviour. It was their *Jesus*!

Someone started to sing, and others joined in. Each person was singing in their own language, but they sensed that they were all singing the same words. It was the words and music from the *Hallelujah Chorus* of Handel's *Messiah*. "King of kings! Lord of lords! He shall reign forever and ever!" They repeated it over and over; and each time they did, the volume increased, until it seemed the whole earth could hear them. This was it! This was the moment that all of history had been wait-ing for. This was the culmination of the great Creator's plan for his creation.

He had, indeed, returned... to judge the earth!

Zion Ben-Jonah Writes

There is something about the return of Jesus that sounds unbelievable to the modern, cynical mind. And yet it is no more unbelievable than any of the other myths and legends (including evolution) that mankind has come up with to explain our existence. Without them, life becomes pointless--a mere accident in an infinite soup of molecules called the universe.

But then, why <u>shouldn't</u> we believe what the Bible has said about the return of Jesus, over any other explanation for life and for our existence? Everything else about the Bible indicates that it is an historically reliable book; and the human race has benefited from it more than it has from any other book that has ever been written. So we would do well to seriously ponder what it has to say about the return of Jesus.

This great event is described in detail by a number of different authors. Paul foretells the Rapture in I Corinthians 15:32-58. He starts by saying, "If the dead rise not, let us eat and drink, for tomorrow we die." And he finishes with these encouraging words: "Know that your labour is not in vain in the Lord." So there <u>is</u> a purpose for our existence. He <u>will</u> return. We <u>will</u> rise again.

Revelation 11:7-13 tells of the death and resurrection of the Two Witnesses, and of the earthquake that hits Jerusalem at the same time. This seventh (last) trumpet marks the start of God's Wrath, or the emptying of the seven vials.

24. New Jerusalem

The opening above the saints grew larger and Rayford felt himself suddenly drawn toward it at great speed. As millions of saints from around the world streamed toward the centre of the glass ceiling those (like Rayford and Chaim) who had arrived first were drawn through the big opening in the ceiling. Rayford looked down and could see clouds below him now. They must be several miles up, and still rising.

Even after they passed through the opening, they continued to rise at a rapid rate, allowing room for what looked like an unending cloud of saints and angels to follow them.

Inside the structure Rayford discovered that there was no sense of up or down. It was like another world, but with total weightlessness. There was no shortage of oxygen, if, indeed, their new bodies were functioning on oxygen at all.

Suddenly Rayford felt guilty. He had become so distracted by the city that he had forgotten about Jesus, the One who had obviously made all of this possible.

"Don't let it bother you!" said someone or something. It was like the voice spoke inside his own head. Nevertheless, Rayford spun around and saw an angel smiling at him. "You'll have plenty of time to meet with the Lord personally," he thought he heard the angel say... although Rayford could not see the man's lips moving.

"Can you...?" Rayford began. But the answer came back before he could finish the sentence.

"That's why I'm here. It's my job to show you around, and to answer your questions."

The two men (for the angel looked to be quite human except for a higher degree of brilliance in his robe and countenance) were still moving at great speed through the vastness of the big city that they had entered only moments earlier. The crowd was thinning out, and it appeared that each saint had been joined by one angelic tour guide.

Rayford's senses were overwhelmed with all that had happened in just a few moments of time. He had been resurrected from what seemed like a deep sleep, returned to perfect health and youth, shot into space without a vehicle or space suit, witnessed momentarily the return of Jesus in the skies above Jerusalem, and then been swept into a whole new world inside a giant glass pyramid, where everything defied the laws of gravity.

"It's approximately fifteen hundred miles high," the angel said, as he read his student's mind. Rayford's head was being filled with information on where he was and what was happening, as quickly as he could process it.

"Millions of saints from around the world have been resurrected and flown here at great speed. Jesus is out there waiting to be seen by each of them before they enter New Jerusalem. Yes, that's the name of this city. We have all been busy preparing for this exciting moment.

"When everyone's inside, by sundown in Israel, we'll gather for the wedding party. No, it won't be dark here. God's presence lights the city constantly. You no longer need to sleep, so the party can go for weeks, in earth time, without let-up.

"The crowd? They'll not be a problem. You'll hear him as clearly as you're hearing me now. There'll be screens if you wish to see him up close, but it's not his body that we worship. It's his Truth and Power. We've planned plenty of music and food and dancing. A lot of celebrating. You don't know how much we up here have been looking forward to this."

"This is just so amazing!" Rayford exclaimed, relieved that his angel had allowed him to express just a tiny bit of what he was feeling.

"We understand your need to express praise," the angel said. "We have the same need ourselves. You'll love the singalongs! It'll be the single greatest act of praise in all history. It really is going to be exciting!"

Rayford had a strange urge to hug his angel, and at that instant his angel reached out to hug him. "Call me Bob," he said, and Rayford registered surprise at such an un-angelic name.

"A bit common, you think?" asked Bob. "Actually, names are not a big deal up here. We never get lost, and people know when they're being addressed personally -- like I'm doing with you right now -- but Bob'll do, if you feel more comfortable using a name."

"Thanks, Bob," Rayford responded. And then his thoughts turned to Irene.

"She's here," Bob reassured him. "You'll see her later. But you'll also come to love everyone here as much as you love her. And the Lord... why, he'll be the greatest love of all!"

Rayford could instantly see the truth in what Bob was saying. On earth he had had a special relationship with Irene; she was his personal responsibility. But here... everyone existed to love and please God. The marriage party, as they called it, was a celebration of their corporate union with God. The euphoria that Rayford had been experiencing since he first rose sleepily up onto his knees there in the Temple Mount enclosure was greater than any pleasure he could ever remember having experienced back on earth, including sex. He did not even *miss* Irene now, or feel impatient about seeing her. He knew instinctively that they were one already... not only with each other, but with all the saints throughout history. They were one in their worship of God. They were entering into a new marriage -- a marriage to God.

Rayford's mind took another turn, and once again Bob turned with him.

"Back on earth?" Bob asked. "They're pretty upset, I can tell you that!" he said with a laugh. "Ol' Dangchao is trying to tell them that we're an alien starship coming to destroy the earth. Guess we are in a way. But he doesn't dare mention God. If he did, maybe they would see the futility of fighting us, and repent.

"Israel's in a mess at the moment. Nearly 7,000 dead already from the quake. But Dangchao is untouched by it. He doesn't think of anyone but himself. Right now he's screaming for military support from every country on earth. Fighter jets, nuclear weapons, rockets, missiles, anything they can find to blow a few holes in our outer shield."

"Can they...?"

"No. Not a chance. It wouldn't matter if they could. The glass isn't really our shield; *God* is. We just put it there for effect. Same with all the gold and precious stones you see everywhere around here. Pretty, isn't it?"

The beautiful structures in New Jerusalem had contributed to Rayford's overall feeling of pleasure. There were perfumes that breathed peace into his spirit too, and a kind of sub-conscious awareness of music humming inside his head. A river of water flowed this way and that through the vast city, but it flowed without banks to hold it in. It was either in a transparent channel, or just held together by its own surface tension. Rayford reached out to touch it. Sure enough, it had no outer covering. It was wet and cold.

There were areas of vegetation that had the feel of jungles without a jungle floor. You could move up, down, or through the beautiful flowers, ferns, vines, and other foliage. Plants tended to lack stalks, although there were beautiful and ornate leaves, and a few vines that laced individual blooms together.

The precious stones that Bob had referred to were more or less strewn along their path. Structures within the glass pyramid were not exactly "buildings" in the sense of a building on earth. There was little need for walls or floors, as people here had nothing to hide, and they were able to view others from above and below as easily as they could from the side. Some semi-transparent structures did serve to separate general areas of the city, so that activities taking place on one side of the walls would not disturb other activities on the other side. Precious stones and plants featured on these partitions.

If there was one thing the saints found difficult about life in New Jerusalem, it was living without their normal concepts of time. You could not talk about "tonight" or "tomorrow" or how many days until something would happen, because there were no nights, and people did not sleep.

They would, however, take time to recline amongst the many gardens, and just soak in the peace and beauty of their new environment from time to time.

In earth days, the marriage party went on for several weeks. Rayford met up with Irene, Elaine, Chloe, Raymie... in fact, all of the original Jesans and the twelve judges. They compared notes on what had happened while they were apart, what their reactions had been when the great resurrection began, and what they had so far learned of life in New Jerusalem.

"We're going to rule the world when the 'battle' is over," Raymie announced. He was twenty-two years old now, and he would continue to age in New Jerusalem until he was approximately thirty. "The assignments," he said, "will be given out after the celebrations."

Rayford prepared them for the possibility that they would have only minor assignments compared to the ones they had carried out during the last seven years. "It always seems that we get slack when we're leading, and God spots the greater faithfulness of humble followers. So we'll probably see some of the little people given the top jobs here," he said.

Neville was there too, and he had some exciting news to announce about something he had learned from his angel.

"You know how we were able to send and receive email without a service provider?" he said. "Well, it was all being processed through a control room up here. This whole place can disappear into another dimension; so it was out there all that time, tapping into the worldwide web to process all of our mail. That's why we never received a bill from Web Wonders after they destroyed it.

"And another thing! It was these guys who vaporised the Web Wonders office, so Dangchao's men couldn't get our files.

"I've been learning so much about how things work up here. It's not magic or anything like that. There are just a lot of laws of physics that people back on earth haven't learned yet. Things like how to overcome gravity and how to read minds. Even our new bodies operate much like our old ones did. Just newer models. They don't need sleep; they don't age, and they're immune to disease. We'll still eat and drink, but most of our power comes from God himself. It comes to us through the Light that fills this pyramid. Outside the pyramid, we would still age, the same as anyone else.

"There's just so much to learn," he exclaimed. "Isn't it great?"

Each saint found delight in something different. Mary loved observing the changes in others now that they were all young and healthy. She found as much pleasure in watching and listening to Neville as he found by what he was learning of divine physics. Just looking at Sheila Armitage and Mary Teresa, who were also thirty years old now, intrigued Mary. Everyone was so beautiful! And so full of energy! She wanted to talk to everyone and to hear their stories about what God had done for them.

Fran, Luis, Mike, and Martin all got into playing games with their new flying skills. They were like little children, although they had to be cautioned a couple of times about the dangers of reckless flying.

Matthew Baker and John Doorman spent a lot of time in the archives, going through videos and other records of their own lives and the lives of others. They were able to gain a better appreciation of what was happening spiritually at various times in their lives. They would locate a time when they prayed for something and then press a button and get an account of what had been the actual effect of the prayer. They were impressed with how God and his angels had managed to work around the intricacies of each person's free will and other natural restrictions that God-had placed on himself.

Reinhard's greatest pleasure was just in wandering around the great city, examining the vegetation, decorations, and some of the strange animal-like creatures that lived there.

There was obviously more than enough to keep everyone fully occupied and fully happy for the next thousand years, which was how long they would be ruling over the world. What was to happen after that, they would worry about when the thousand years were drawing to a close. But in the meantime, they would all have duties to perform in ruling the world under the guidance of Jesus and his angels for the next thousand years.

Even while they were celebrating, God was pouring out his "Wrath" on the world below. All the suffering that the saints had just been through was nothing compared to what was happening outside at that time. The armies of the world were gathering their forces together for one final assault on New Jerusalem. Dangchao had a plan to fly nuclear weapons in through the same opening that the saints had used. But the saints were going to join with the angels in blocking that assault... known as the Battle of Armageddon.

Zion Ben-Jonah Writes

Revelation 21 gives a detailed description of the New Jerusalem after it actually lands on the earth (i.e. after the battle of Armageddon).

We have not bothered in this book to detail the gore that accompanies the "seven vials" of the Wrath. You can read about it in The Revelation, chapter 16. Unfortunately, despite all that God does to get their attention, the world still does not repent. Instead, they become more bitter against him. They eventually unite in a fierce war against God himself. (See the next chapter.)

The Bible tells us that there will be no marriage in heaven. (Matthew 22:30, Mark 12:25 and Luke 20:34.) This is a bit hard for most people to imagine, as marriage seems to be the closest to heaven that most of us ever experience here on earth (although some would say it is the closest to hell too!) However, just as we cannot fathom how God could do many of the things that he _has_ done (e.g. Creation itself), so it is hard for us to comprehend the far greater pleasures that he is yet to give to those who put their faith in him.

The Bible tells us that God will provide the Light in New Jerusalem. The physical presence of Jesus, ministering to millions of different individuals is hard to picture. But through the combined assistance of the Light (God's spiritual presence) and his heavenly hosts (the angels), Jesus will apparently be able to meet the needs of all his faithful followers without any problems.

25. Armageddon

The Battle of Armageddon itself was really just the start of another story. The troops on earth, it turned out, had been gathering for over a year by the time the attack began. Dangchao had sensed that a showdown was coming, and he had secretly ordered manoeuvres to begin even before Rayford and Chaim had left London and Sydney for Jersualem.

The appearance of New Jerusalem in the skies over the Middle East merely gave Dangchao a *target* against which to hurl the best (or worst, depending on your perspective) that his world had to offer. He had convinced the various governments of the United Nations that the apparition in the skies over the Middle East was part of an invasion by aliens from another solar system. The survival of the human race, he said, depended on wiping out or at least repelling these intruders -- who were blamed for everything from the asteroid and subsequent tidal wave to the stinging locusts that Dangchao himself had unleashed.

The mile-wide opening in the glass base of the pyramid directly over Jerusalem had never been closed after that first official opening to let Jesus and his army of angels through. It was, from Dangchao's perspective, the obvious place to start his strike against the forces of God.

Dangchao, as commander-in-chief of the mighty armies of the world, loaded up all of the world's best fighter jets with nuclear weapons. If even a *few* of his pilots were able to actually fly through the opening, then they could drop a bit of his hell inside their heaven. And if that failed, he had imported virtually every available ground-to-air missile on earth to the state of Israel, and he had built launching sites for them all over the country, so that they could all be fired at the new world of the saints whenever he gave the signal.

Near the end of the marriage celebrations in New Jerusalem, the saints had been instructed on how they were to defend their city. They were to engage the enemy without any weapons of defence, only God's presence... and the truth. Each saint was to spend a number of hours simply bathing in the Light of New Jerusalem, which was very much like sun-bathing on earth... but not as hot. They would soak up enough power to enable them to function wisely once outside New Jerusalem. But they were also seriously instructed on the need to follow their angels implicitly and without question in every move that they made.

Then, when the time came, the saints and angels were sent out to meet the approaching squadrons. Christ himself was stationed just below the opening. His brilliance was so powerful that it was visible for many miles in all directions. He was an unmistakable target for each of the enemy planes... and a public taunt to Dangchao.

The saints and angels were able to fly at supersonic speed. Some zoomed down to confront the approaching jets. Then they swung around to match the flight path. They were positioned all around (above, below, and in front of) the jets as they both sped toward the opening.

"You don't really want to do this," one of the saints would communicate (or words to this effect) to the plane's pilot by thought transference. "We're not here to hurt you," they would continue. "Save yourself and your world by turning back now." "God loves you." "He does not want to see you die." The messages were fired into each cockpit, and into the minds of every crew member on the larger planes. Some of the saints and angels were visible outside the aircraft as well.

But each time they did this, the hardened, puppets of the Antichrist system would convince themselves that they were being mentally assaulted by the heavenly beings. They would manoeuvre their planes in an attempt to fire weapons at the saints. Rockets flew in all directions as jets veered off course and out of formation. While they were firing at the creatures that they could see outside their windows, some of them accidentally shot down allied planes in the vicinity. Some planes executed impossible twists, turns, and backflips to either shake or break the armies of New Jerusalem. Many of them went out of control as a result, crashing to earth with their deadly cargoes.

They were literally blowing themselves out of the skies in their insane resistance to God's final call to repentance. Not one of them responded to the offers of peace being made by the saints.

Meanwhile, on the ground, Dangchao gave the order for the missiles to be launched. But another larger wing of the heavenly army had already reached the launch sites. Saints and angels were seen by closed circuit TV, hovering over the missiles, and seen personally appearing outside windows, and flying down hallways and into otherwise secure rooms where the orders to press buttons were to be carried out. With help from the internet experts in New Jerusalem, a few of the saints were even able to appear on computer monitors in the control rooms and talk to the workers.

(During the Rapture, similar technology had been used to put close-up footage of Jesus above Jerusalem into television receivers all over the world.)

The messages of love, peace, and a call to repentance were transmitted to everyone involved in the Battle; and again the messages were rejected. Instead, the earthly armies reacted in confusion. Staff turned from their duties in an effort to stop the intruders. Weapons were used, but, because the saints could move at speeds many times faster than their attackers, the weapons were useless. The saints had the reflexes and flying skills of houseflies. Attempts by Dangchao's servants to shoot them often resulted in deaths and casualties to their own personnel.

It was in the middle of all this confusion that Dangchao gave the order for all of the missiles to be fired. It was too soon. The fighter squadrons had not yet returned from their assault. Consequently, allied planes which had not already destroyed themselves were destroyed by "friendly" missiles, if there can be such things.

Many missiles were never launched, simply because the people responsible for launching them had been distracted, killed, or injured in the melee. The saints succeeded in pulling plugs on some and altering the settings on others, causing some missiles to veer off target. These did little more than bounce off the glass shield, causing more destruction to the earth, some five miles below the base of the huge city, than they did to New Jerusalem itself.

The saints stayed very close to their angels, who could sense ahead of time when it was best to leave their assigned sphere of operation and head for safer climes, or to just return to New Jerusalem. In this way, they were able to escape areas that were later fired on by Dangchao's own troops.

Contrary to Rayford's theory about both sides suffering losses during a war, the Battle of Armageddon was as one-sided as any war that has ever been fought. The heavenly armies reported not a single casualty. It was not that they were immune to the weapons being fired at them, but only that they could not fail to escape injury if they would just faithfully *follow directions*. This, of course, was the lesson that had been missed by the inhabitants of Earth for most of their existence. Each time God would tell them something, they would take the first opportunity to forget it, and to do things in their own way. Now the world was witnessing what could be achieved with an army of people who knew what it was to obey God.

The angels appeared to be more infallible and more indestructible than the saints themselves, and so the saints just needed to stay perfectly in tune with their angels and they would find themselves to always be in the right place at the right time... which is exactly what they did.

After the battle, the saints spent several months cleaning up the remnants of the war on the area of the earth's surface that would be covered by New Jerusalem. There were no survivors in Israel itself, but neighbouring countries needed to be evacuated. The saints supervised the evacuations too. They also had the job of soaking up all radiation, which they were able to do using technology that was available in New Jerusalem.

When all was ready, the entire paper-thin floor of the big city slid back and turned up on its sides to make a very thick wall that was over 200 feet high on all four sides. Each side had three huge gates which were always kept open.

With the floor folded back, the city was able to

descend the remaining five miles to the earth's surface, and then mould itself to the contours of that part of the earth.

For the next thousand years, the saints would rule the world -- that is, those who had survived the Wrath of God, and their descendants -- from within New Jerusalem. Emissaries would come and go from the holy city from time to time, as they checked up on progress around the world, but for the most part, those outside the city were on their own, experiencing a kind of purgatory as they struggled to learn from those who had earned the right to rule.

The job of the saints was to teach the nations of the world how to live in peace, how to serve one another in love, how to share the earth's resources equally, how to live without money, and most of all, how to live in harmony with God himself -- asking for, listening to, and heeding his instructions in all matters of life.

The saints were guided in their duties by the angels; but also they were guided by what they had already learned (and were continuing to learn) from the teachings of Jesus -- God's only begotten Son, and God's perfect revelation of himself to human kind. He was not only their Saviour, but also their Lord and Master.

And that is how it should be.

For a more detailed explanation of Bible prophecies and how they relate to world events today, please send for our book, <u>Armageddon for Beginners</u> A small donation to help with postage and printing costs would be appreciated.

Write to:

Jesus Christians

Box A678
Sydney South 1235
Australia

Box 580
Guildford GU1 1GR
United Kingdom

Box 8617
Thiruvanmiyur
Chennai, 600041
South India

email: fold@idl.net.au
internet: www.jesuschristians.com